AFRAID OF THE BWGAN-WOOD?

WHO'S AFRAID OF THE BWGAN-WOOD?

Anne Lewis

Illustrated by
Sarah Warburton

HONNO CHILDREN'S FICTION

Published by Honno
'Ailsa Craig', Heol y Cawl, Dinas Powys,
Bro Morgannwg, CF6 4AH

First Impression 1995

Reprinted 1996, 2000, 2002, 2004, 2008

British Library Cataloguing in Publication Data

A catalogue record for this book is available from the British Library

ISBN 1 870206 14 2

Published with the financial support
of the Arts Council of Wales

Cover illustration by Sarah Warburton
Cover design by Olwen Fowler

Typeset and printed in Wales by Dinefwr Press, Llandybïe

For the children of Ysgol y Borth,
who made me start thinking about Bwganod.

For Ellie, who insisted.

For Denise and Dan, who made all the difference.

1

The Bwgan-wood

All day long, people hurry to and fro across the waste ground on the fringes of the Bwgan-wood.

The waste ground itself used to be an ironworks, and if you poke about amongst the slag heaps and the rubbish tips you can still find fallen-down sheds and very old, rusty machinery and bits of railway tracking all smothered in ivy and brambles and long grass. The whole place is so neglected and overgrown and so full of smelly rubbish that hardly anybody goes there any more.

But the footpath along the edge of the waste ground is a useful short cut between the Old Village and the big new estate on the hill, and people use it a lot. In the mornings there are grown-ups on their way to work, and older children hurrying to school. Later in the day there'll be mothers with pushchairs and shopping, and people going jogging, or walking their dogs. On Saturdays gangs of kids roam the waste land and make secret dens in amongst the brambles. And in summer-time people even wander into the Bwgan-wood itself and have picnics on the grass.

Nobody sees the eyes peeping out at them from the tangles of the trees. Nobody notices the way the leaves sometimes shake and shiver when there isn't any wind. Nobody has the faintest idea that they are being *watched*.

And nobody hears the laughter …

Once dusk has fallen, the waste land is empty and silent. Humans don't like using the short cut after dark. People say it's because there aren't any lights on the path, and that you could trip over and hurt yourself, or even wander off the path altogether and get lost in the Wood. All of this is perfectly true. But it's not the real reason.

The real reason is that it's creepy in the waste land at night. So creepy, and so weird, that even grown-up humans have enough sense to stay away.

The children say the Wood is haunted. They tell each other all sorts of stories about the ghosts and the monsters who are supposed to lurk amongst the trees when it starts to get dark. Nearly all the stories are complete rubbish, and just made up to scare people. But the children are right about one thing.

Dusk is when the mischief starts …

2

Dusk

It was a fine, warm evening right at the beginning of the Autumn term. Since about a quarter to seven, Ebenezer Terrace had been jam-packed solid with parked cars and crowds of grown-ups waiting. Then, at exactly seven o'clock, the door at the top of the steps swung open and all the Brownies surged out of Ebenezer Chapel vestry in a chattering flood. Thirty seconds later all the Cub Scouts burst out of the Memorial Hall next door and raced yelling along the path to the road. For a little while there was pandemonium in Ebenezer Terrace – everybody shouting and waving and dodging round everybody else to get to the cars; doors slamming, engines revving up and indicator lights flashing.

In amongst all the fuss and commotion the five children from Mostyn Close made their way to the Chapel gates, as they always did, and stood there in a bunch to wait for their lift. The Mostyn Close parents had a rota for dropping the children off at Cub Scouts and Brownies and picking them up afterwards – and tonight it was Warren's father's turn to take them all home.

'Isn't he here yet?' said Sally-Ann, stretching on tiptoes to see past the crowd.

David had climbed up onto the wall, to get a better view.

'Give him a chance, willya? It's like a fairground out there.'

One by one the parked cars began to move away from

the kerb, and other cars pulled in to take their place. The children watched anxiously, but there was still no sign of Warren's father's blue van.

'I wish he'd hurry up,' said Bethan grumpily. 'I want to go home!'

'Aw, stop fussing,' said Warren. 'He'll *be* here, okay?'

More cars were leaving. The street was getting emptier. And Warren's father still hadn't turned up.

One of the parents they knew wound his car window down and called across to them.

'Any of you kids want a lift?'

'We're okay, thanks,' Warren said. 'We're waiting for my dad.'

The man nodded and drove off.

The children waited, fidgeting and kicking the heels of their shoes against the steps. They watched as the last of the cars drove off down the road. They watched the last little groups of people disappear around the corner, and heard the voices and the footsteps fade away into silence.

All at once Ebenezer Terrace was empty, and very, very quiet.

The sun had slipped down behind the huge stone bulk of the chapel, and the street was suddenly chilly and full of gloomy shadows. The windows of the houses opposite began to look like a row of big, shocked eyes glaring at the children. All the front doors were shut, and nobody went in or out.

Bethan shivered. 'I don't like it now everybody's gone. It's creepy.'

'What if he's forgotten all about us?' said Eleri. 'What if we have to stay here all night, and when the policeman comes round in the morning we'll all be frozen to death?'

'Oh, no!' Bethan started to cry. 'I want to go home! I want to go home *now*!'

Because he was worried, Warren lost his temper.

'Don't be so *stupid*, the pair of you! He's been held up, that's all. Traffic jam, or a puncture, or something. Just keep your hair on, okay?'

'Anyway,' said Sally-Ann, 'It's only September. Nobody freezes to death in September, do they?'

David glanced at his birthday watch and made it play 'The Return of the Jedi'. (It had a calculator, and played fifteen tunes, and was just new enough not to have driven everybody stark raving mad. Yet.)

'Seven-sixteen,' he said. 'Your dad ought to have got here by now, Woz. He's not normally this late, is he?'

Warren was still snappish. 'Well, it's not my fault, is it? Nothing to do with me. Perhaps he got called out on a job, or something. I don't know, do I?' Warren's father was a plumber, and often had to go out again after work to deal with emergencies like burst pipes.

'Something must have gone wrong,' said David.

'What if there's been an accident?' said Eleri.

Sally-Ann jumped down from the wall where she'd been perching. 'Right. That settles it. I'm going to phone my mam. Anybody got ten pee?'

They all crowded into the phone box at the end of the terrace. But the phone had been vandalised, and the money wouldn't go in. After trying and trying, Sally-Ann put down the receiver with a bang.

'Now what?'

'We'll just have to walk, that's all,' said David, and everybody's heart sank.

There were two ways of getting from Ebenezer Terrace to the new estate on the hill. You could go down through the Old Village to the main road, and then along the industrial estate and past the council houses and over the big new road bridge (where the little River Ceirw joined the bigger, dirtier river of the main valley), then past more council houses and the primary school and up the High Street of Nant-y-Ceirw New Town through some very busy road junctions until you finally got to the narrow winding lane which led to the estate on its hill. That was the way the cars went, but if you were walking it took forever.

The other way was the short cut through the waste land which people called the Old Ironworks. If you hurried, it took fifteen minutes.

'We could go the short way,' Sally-Ann said. 'It won't be dark till half-past eightish.' But you could tell she wasn't keen.

'My mum'd go spare,' said David. 'I'm not allowed down the Old Ironworks on my own. Dad says there's too many nutters about.'

'Well, I'm not going down there, not at this time of night,' Eleri declared. And for once, everybody agreed with her.

'Better start the long way, then,' said Warren glumly. 'Perhaps we'll meet my dad on the way.'

Feeling thoroughly disgruntled, they started off in the direction of the square. But suddenly Bethan tugged Sally-Ann to a halt. She'd stopped snivelling, and was grinning all over her face.

'No – wait. I just remembered. We won't have to walk. We can phone from Sharon's shop.'

Sharon was Bethan's grown-up sister. She worked at the little supermarket in Williams Terrace, just two streets down from where they were.

Everybody stared.

'But she won't be there now, will she?' Sally-Ann pointed out. 'All the shops closed hours ago.'

'Yes, she will. They don't shut till half-past seven on a Friday. My mam said if ever we were stuck for a lift we had to go and see Sharon.'

There was a moment of dead silence. Then everybody screeched, '*Bethan*!'

'Why didn't you tell us before?' said Warren.

Bethan went red. 'I forgot,' she admitted.

'*Forgot*? You'll forget your own name next!' said Sally-Ann in disgust.

'Honestly, Bethan Parry, you need your head read,' said Warren.

'We could've been there all this time,' Eleri wailed. 'We could've bought sweets ... gobstoppers and sherbet dips ...' David looked at his watch. 'Never mind about the sherbet dips. We've got three minutes to get there. C'mon!'

3

Mischief

They ran all the way.

Luckily the shop was still open, and there were even a few customers still inside. Sharon was at the checkout, tapping the buttons on the till so fast that all you could see on the display was a flickering green blur.

She was very glad to see them: so glad and so relieved that of course the very first thing she did was scold.

'Where've you *been*? I was worried sick!' She paused to smile politely at her customer, and give him his change, then she glared at Sally-Ann.

'I thought *you'd* have enough sense to come straight down here when Warren's father didn't show up. What kept you?'

Sally-Ann made a face at Bethan, who hung her head. 'We didn't know you were still open.'

'Typical,' said Sharon, and began checking-out her next customer's shopping. 'Warren's dad rang up. He had to go out to fix a burst boiler, and everybody else was tied up. I would have come to fetch you myself, only I'm on my own here tonight, and we were busy ... That'll be seven pounds forty-nine pee, please, Mrs Thomas ... Thank you ... Goodnight! ... So if you kids'll give me a hand with the clearing up, we'll get home that much quicker.'

When the customers had gone the children helped Sharon carry the fruit and vegetables from the outside stands into the store-room at the back of the shop. David swept the floor with the extra-wide brush. They all helped stack the empty boxes and rubbish outside in the yard for the bin man while Sharon was counting the till money and locking it up in the safe. By the time all the jobs were finished, it was eight o'clock.

'Not to worry,' Sharon said as she locked the door. 'We'll take the short cut and be home in no time. Come on!'

Nobody moved. Instead, they all looked at one another.

'Uh … the short cut?' said Warren.

'We've got to *walk*?' said Bethan. 'Where's your car, Shar?'

'In the garage, having its MOT,' said Sharon. 'What's the matter, forgotten how to use your legs?'

'I don't want to go the short way,' Eleri said in a frightened voice. 'Oh, please, Sharon, don't let's go the short way.'

Sharon was tired. The last thing she wanted just then was an argument about how to get home.

'Oh, for Heaven's sake,' she snapped. 'What's the matter with you all? There's nothing wrong with the short cut, okay? It won't be dark for another half-hour at least.'

'I'm not scared of the Old Ironworks, even if you lot are,' Sally-Ann said smugly. She felt a whole lot braver now that there was a grown-up with them.

Warren glared at Sally-Ann and said 'Me neither,' in case anybody thought he was a wimp.

'Right then,' said Sharon. 'Quick march, and no more nonsense.'

She led the way at a brisk walk, so that the children had to trot and skip to keep up.

It was a lovely evening. The sky was still light, and covered in little gold-and-crimson clouds. A few bright stars shone in the blueness between.

'Planets,' said Sally-Ann knowledgeably.

'Red sky at night, shepherd's delight,' said Bethan.

9

The gate that led to the Old Ironworks was old and rusty. It screeched and groaned as Sharon tugged it open – 'Like a horror film,' said David, sniggering.

'Thanks very much, David,' said Sharon. 'Okay, you lot. Let's go.'

Everybody filed through, except Eleri. She hung back, gripping the railings and suddenly looking stubborn and frightened.

'I'm not going down there,' she panted. 'There's ghosts, and robbers, and boogy-boos and things in the Old Ironworks. Oh, Sharon, *please* don't make me go down there!' She sounded really scared.

Sharon took a deep breath and looked as though she was praying silently for patience. 'There's no such thing as ghosts, Eleri. You should know that, at your age. No robbers, no boogy-boos or anything like that. All we'll meet on the path tonight are people walking their dogs. Understand?'

'Boogy-boos,' Warren sneered. 'Grow up, Eleri. Take no notice of her, Sharon, she's always making up stories to scare people.'

'I'm not! I'm not! And there *are* boogy-boos down in the Old Ironworks. My Nan *saw* them! So there!'

'Oooh!' said Bethan, round-eyed. Even David looked worried for a moment.

'Garbage,' said Warren. 'Your Nan's dippy, if you ask me.'

Eleri went bright red. 'She isn't! Don't you *dare* say my Nan's dippy, Warren Davies! Don't you *ever* say things like that about my Nan!'

Sharon was really angry now. 'That's enough, both of you! One more word out of either of you and I'll tell your mothers. We're going the short way home, and we're going *now*. Got it?'

They followed her through the gate in silence.

Sharon had been quite right: on a lovely evening like this lots of people were out walking their dogs through the waste land. Before they'd gone very far down the path they met one of their teachers with his huge, friendly Saint Bernard dog. A bit further on two spaniels came dashing out of the undergrowth and scampered up to say hello before being whistled back by their owner. And near the bottom of the slope they met two ladies with nine puppies on leads. When the puppies saw the children they went crazy with delight and jumped up and yapped and thrashed their little tails about and tried to lick the children's faces when they bent down to stroke them. They were so enchanting that even Sharon found it hard to tear herself away.

The light seemed to have faded very quickly while they'd been playing with the puppies. Out on the open hillside, amongst the buddleia bushes and the bright tussocks of golden grass, nobody had noticed the change – but now their path began to wind in amongst trees and thick undergrowth, and suddenly it was almost dark. They were inside the Wood.

Here everything was hushed and still. Underfoot, the path shone whitely between crowding trees and the dense gloom of tall bushes beyond.

Sharon's voice came loudly out of the darkness, making them all jump.

'Come on, get a move on. Not far now!'

Just here the path was too narrow for everybody to walk in a bunch, so they had to spread out. Warren had picked up a big stick: armed with this, he felt a lot braver, so he and David went on in front. Sally-Ann and Eleri came next, with Sharon and Bethan just behind them.

'I don't like this, Sharon,' Bethan whimpered. 'It's creepy!'

Sharon spoke loudly on purpose so that everybody could hear.

'Don't be silly, Bethan. There's nothing to be afraid of. There are birds and hedgehogs and little rabbits all around us. They're not scared, so why should we be? It's just a bit darker than we're used to, that's all.'

They walked on. Sally-Ann glanced back over her shoulder – but Bethan and Sharon were talking in low voices and not close enough to hear. So she leaned across to whisper to Eleri.

'Did your Nan *really* see boogy-boos down here, in the dark like this?'

Eleri had been daydreaming about having a puppy of her own. Sally-Ann's whisper made her jump, so instead of whispering back she answered quite loudly.

'They're not boogy-boos, not really. They're bwganod. Boo-GAN-odd. That's their proper name.'

There was a sudden, sharp rustle in the branches overhead.

'Squirrel, or a bird,' Sharon said quickly, before anybody could panic. 'Keep going. Nearly at the foot-bridge now.'

The dusk deepened around them. The wood *was* creepy, whatever Sharon said. There were faint, furtive rustling sounds in the bushes alongside. Perhaps they were just rabbits and hedgehogs – but then again, what if they weren't …?

'*What's that?*' Eleri gasped – and everybody jumped.

Sharon squinted upwards in the gloom, to where Eleri was pointing.

'It's a dead leaf, Eleri. It's falling off a tree. Leaves do that in the autumn, in case you hadn't noticed. Keep moving, all of you.'

The children eyed Eleri's floating leaves as they passed. They were just pale shapes in the dimness, too high up to

12

see clearly – but surely leaves shouldn't float around in mid air like that? Or follow them as they walked?

Sally-Ann yelped – an acorn had fallen on her head. Another one fell on Bethan and made her squeal. Everybody began to walk faster.

Suddenly there was a shout from up ahead and a crashing noise. Next moment David and Warren were hurtling back towards Sharon and the girls. It was just light enough to see their faces. Their eyes were as round as dinner plates.

'What's the matter *now*?' said Sharon nastily.

'M-my stick!' Warren gasped. 'It – it got taken off me!'

'What d'you mean, got taken off you? David, what happened?'

David took a deep breath. 'He was bashing the bushes with his stick – and then, all of a sudden, it *went*!'

'Went where?'

Warren shuddered. 'It was like … like somebody snatched it out of my hand!'

'Then it swung round and hit him!' David said.

Everybody stood very still, their hearts thumping. The only sound was Bethan making scared little whimpering noises. Sharon strode to the bend in the path.

'Anybody there?'

There was no answer – not even a rustle.

'This is ridiculous,' Sharon declared angrily. 'Your stick must have got tangled up in the brambles, and when you let go, it jerked back and hit you. I don't know what's got into you kids tonight, I really d …'

As she was talking, there was a sudden, loud shivering of twigs overhead and the next moment a shower of dead leaves and dry moss and little stones and feathers had descended on Sharon's head, exactly as though somebody had emptied a rubbish bin. The last thing to fall was an old bird's nest. It stuck on Sharon's head like a hat.

13

Sharon ducked – too late – and gave a shriek. 'Ow! Urgh! What a mess!'

Everybody froze.

Sharon flung the nest away and started furiously brushing twigs and feathers out of her hair and off her coat.

'Well, don't just stand there! Give me a hand with all this rubbish! Blasted squirrels!'

'Is that what it was?' said Sally-Ann in a small voice. 'Squirrels?'

'Of course it was squirrels! What else could it have been? Squirrels are always knocking over old birds' nests, it's a well-known fact.'

'Oh,' said Bethan. Everybody started breathing again.

'You looked like Guy Fawkes, Sharon,' said Sally-Ann, and gave a shaky giggle. Now that they'd come up with a reasonable explanation, Sharon getting hit over the head with a bird's nest began to seem funny instead of scary.

'Poor old squirrel,' said Warren. 'It took one look at Sharon and got so scared it nearly fell out of the tree!'

Even Bethan was laughing now. 'Penny for the Guy!' she chanted. 'Who's got a penny for the horrible scruffy old Guy?'

'You cheeky lot,' said Sharon. 'I'll give you penny for the Guy!' She grabbed the bird's nest and threw it at Warren. Bethan, Warren and Sally-Ann shrieked and ran giggling down the path with Sharon in pursuit.

David and Eleri stayed where they were, perfectly still, and looked at one another. Because at the moment when Sharon had yelled 'Ow!' they'd both seen something moving in the branches overhead. Two somethings – both misty-pale, and shimmering with a strange purple light. And then they'd heard, quite distinctly, a burst of echoing, mischievous laughter.

Not squirrels. Definitely not squirrels.

They should both have been scared out of their wits – but they weren't. They just felt awed, and breathless with an excitement that was very nearly fear, but not quite.

Human squeals drifted back through the wood as Sharon caught up with the other three and stuffed grass down the back of Warren's jumper. Eleri and David walked slowly towards the noise. They kept looking upwards, and from side to side – but the pale shapes had vanished.

'Those boogy-boos your Nan saw ...' David said quietly.

'Bwganod,' said Eleri. 'That's what they're really called.'

'You reckon that's what those were, then?'

Eleri nodded, so full of wonder she could hardly speak. 'We saw *bwganod*. Bwganod are *real* ...'

'Yeah.' David grinned suddenly. 'Wow. Nobody else saw them, though. Just us. Trouble is, nobody'd believe us. They'd think we were crackers.'

15

Eleri tried to remember what her Nan had told her about bwganod.

'They weren't scary at all … not really. More sort of … mischievous. Playing tricks …'

'They didn't *sound* scary, either. Weird, but not horrible, know what I mean?'

Eleri said slowly, 'They sounded like … children …'

They trudged on. In the distance they could see golden sunset light between the trees, and Sharon and the others waiting for them by the foot-bridge. Sally-Ann waved and called, and Eleri waved back.

'Are they ghosts, or what?' said David, still thinking about bwganod.

Eleri shook her head decisively. 'No. Ghosts are dead people. Nan says bwganod are alive. She reckons they've been here longer than humans. In the olden days they used to play tricks on people, and turn into scary shapes to frighten them.'

David chuckled. 'That figures, doesn't it?'

Sharon was shouting and making hurry-up gestures from the end of the path. 'Come on, you two. We'll never get home at this rate.'

David and Eleri started to run.

'If they'd really *wanted* to frighten us,' Eleri grinned, 'they could've turned into big white scary things with huge eyes and hair all sticking up, and they'd have gone 'Aaaaarghhh!' But they didn't …'

And then it happened.

'AAAAARGHHHH!!!' screeched a voice, horribly loud and close – and a white wavering THING came swooping low over Eleri's shoulder and down the path towards the rest of the group.

Everybody's heart stopped.

And suddenly they were all running – Eleri and David

and Bethan and Warren and Sally-Ann – running in sheer blind panic, faster than they'd ever run in their whole lives before.

'Stop! Come back! It's only an old owl!' Sharon yelled as David and Eleri dashed past – but nobody heard her. Panic had taken over. It was as though all five had suddenly reached snapping point: they'd had as much as they could take of gloom and creepiness and mysterious happenings, and this fright was the last straw. Everybody had had the same overwhelming urge at the same moment: to get out of this horrible, scary wood and back to the familiar lights and warmth and safety of the estate.

They pounded across the foot-bridge and charged through the bushes on the far side. Without even pausing for breath they pelted through the ruins of the old railway yard and on up the hillside to the gate. Nobody stopped running until they were finally under the street lights of Mostyn Close.

4

Bwganod

The noise of the gate opening echoed faintly but clearly across the waste land. A few minutes later there was a second groaning screech as Sharon went through, and a clang as she shut it behind her. Voices were raised in the distance; then they too faded away.

The Old Ironworks was silent and still in the dusk. Humans and dogs had all gone home.

Then the eyes which had been watching the children blinked a few times. The bushes at the side of the bridge rustled slightly. And two misty-pale shapes like wisps of cloud – faintly tinted with different colours, and shimmering at the edges with a strange purple light – rose silently out of the undergrowth and drifted upwards.

When they came to rest in the branches above the river, the mists shrank and got more and more solid and harder to see through until they turned into Tati-bwgan and Bwgan-daio.

Bwgan-daio's eyes were round and scared.

'Have they gone yet? All of them?'

Tati-bwgan floated above the tree-tops until she could see the path in both directions.

'Every last one,' she reported. 'And the gates are shut.'

Daio sighed with relief. The tricks they'd been playing had been against the Rules – and Daio was a worrier.

'We'll get caught one of these days,' he said. 'And then what?'

Tati's face was alight with mischief. 'Don't be such a

misery-guts. Nobody's ever around to see. And *They* can't see us at all.'

'One of *Them* knew about us, though. I heard them talking.'

Tati shrugged. 'So what? Anyway, you were laughing as much as I was when we tipped that old nest onto the big girl's head.'

Daio giggled in spite of himself. 'The look on her face! And wasn't it funny when Tiw said hello and they all ran away?'

That had been the funniest thing of all. Bwganod can see in the dark, so Tati and Daio hadn't missed a thing. The more they thought about the heavy, clumsy humans galumphing away down the path, squeaking with fright – and the puzzled look the owl had given them before shrugging and swooping away – the funnier it became. Now that they were alone, and didn't have to be careful, Tati and Daio laughed out loud until their insides ached.

'*Wicked!*' Daio gasped. 'And the best bit is – we didn't actually do a thing! It was Tiw who got them really scared! And she's just an owl!'

Tati sniffed. 'We could've scared them *much* worse than that, if we'd wanted to.'

'I know. But we're not allowed. So don't even think about it, Tat.'

'Stupid old Rules,' Tati grumbled. 'Bet I could have scared them worse than you, though.'

'Bet you couldn't.'

'Oh, yeah? Watch this.'

The shimmering, purplish edges of Tati swelled up and changed colour – and all at once she was a huge scaly monster with blood dripping from her fangs.

'Pathetic,' scoffed Daio – and changed himself into a great big bloodshot eyeball, with claws.

The monster snarled horribly, and breathed out unreal fire. Then it opened its mouth wider and wider until all its insides spilled out. The dreadful apparition shimmered and shrank – and there was Tati again, in her normal shape.

'Not bad,' said the eyeball grudgingly.

'C'mon,' said Tati. 'Let's go and see Tiw.'

They found the barn owl perched on top of a derelict chimney among the ruins of the old foundry.

'Hi, Tiw,' said Daio cheerfully.

'What? Oh – hello,' the owl said. She was staring intently at the ground far below, watching with her keen night-vision for tiny movements in the long grass.

'Fancy a game, Tiw?' said Tati.

'Well, actually,' Tiw said apologetically, 'I'm a bit – er …' She stiffened. 'Ah. Excuse me,' and a millisecond later she was gone.

Looking down, Tati and Daio saw the silent feathered bullet that was Tiw streaking at incredible speed into the tangled grass. At the very last instant she braked: the huge taloned feet shot out, the big wings rowed the air without a sound – and a moment later she was sitting in a tree twenty yards away with a mouse in her beak. Tati and Daio could see the tail quite clearly in the moonlight. Tiw turned away politely while she swallowed it, head first.

'I wish she wouldn't do that,' Daio said, shuddering.

'What, disappear all the time?'

'No. The mice. I *like* mice.'

'She's got to eat, like everybody else,' said Tati wisely. 'If she didn't, we'd be up to the eyeballs in them, and everybody else would starve.'

They knew there was no point in hanging around while Tiw was hunting. Instead, the two bwganod drifted away to where the little Ceirw River tumbled in waterfalls down the steep cliffs at the furthest end of the Old Ironworks.

Above the cliffs was the secret valley and the woods where their family lived.

'Wonder if Eldan's back yet?' Tati remarked as they flew.

Daio made a face. 'Shouldn't think so. We could ask around, I suppose.'

Eldan was a special friend of theirs, and great fun to be with – but there was a snag. He was one of the Tylwyth Teg, whom some people call the Elves, or the Fair Folk, or the Children of the Sidhe. Anybody who knows Elves will tell you that you can't rely on them to stay in one place for long. They're here one moment and gone the next, and no one, least of all the Elves themselves, knows when or where they'll turn up again.

Three nights ago the Ceirw Valley had echoed with their music and their laughter and glimmered with the light that shines out of their golden hair. Tonight everywhere was dark and silent. Tati and Daio knew from experience that Eldan could be away for a week, or a year, or twenty years. They also knew that whenever he did appear again, he'd carry on with a conversation, or a game, or a song at the exact point where he'd left it – and he didn't seem to understand when you tried to explain that Time had passed, and a lot of other things had happened in between. He just thought you were teasing him.

'Bwgantaid says their Time is different from ours,' said Daio.

Tati frowned. 'I don't see how it can be, do you? I mean, Time is just Time, isn't it?'

'It's because they exist in a lot of different worlds at once, Bwgantaid says.'

Tati thought about it, and gave up in disgust. 'Sounds loopy to me.'

By now they'd reached their grandparents' Bwganhouse. Their grandfather was outside, puffing at his pipe and looking gloomy.

'Slung out of my own house,' he grumbled, 'with a list of jobs to do as long as your arm ...'

'Why, what's Naino doing?'

'Making new pillows.'

Their faces fell. 'Oh, no!'

Making fresh pillows out of willowherb fluff was something Bwgan-naino did every autumn – and it was the messiest, fiddliest, tickliest job you could possibly imagine. You had to pick out all the tiny seeds one by one, and the fluff got up your nose and made you sneeze.

'Why does she bother?' Daio said. 'She doesn't have to!' In their Bwganhouse, they managed perfectly well without any pillows at all.

'Try telling Them that,' said Bwgantaid sourly – meaning Naino and her Bwganhouse.

Bwgan-naino was one of those people who can't bear to be without anything to do. If she wasn't cleaning, she was baking, and if she wasn't baking she was brewing or knitting or sewing or mending things or, as at present, making willowherb pillows.

'*And* one of them foreign quilt things, to go on the bed,' Bwgantaid said gloomily. 'I wish I'd never asked them Norwegian Kobolds to stay last summer, I'm telling you straight.'

Tati and Daio fidgeted a bit, and glanced sideways at each other.

'Well – um – better be going, I suppose,' said Tati hastily.

'See you later, Taid,' said Daio. 'Tell Naino we called.'

And rather guiltily, they made their escape.

'We could've stayed to help, I suppose,' said Daio.

'No way,' Tati said firmly. 'Last time I helped Naino with pillows, I sneezed for a whole week.'

Nobody in the Ceirw woods had seen Eldan or his family. Tati and Daio floated rather disconsolately back down the cliffs to the Old Ironworks.

As they were skirting the smelly patch of oily swamp near the old railway yard, they almost fell over Gwrach y Rhibyn who had crawled out of her pool and was snuffling along the path. She was covered in mud and slime, and duckweed dripped from her long green hair.

'Watch where you're going, can't you?'

'Sorry,' they said together, and backed hastily out of her way. Gwrach y Rhibyn was a powerful witch and it wasn't wise to upset her.

'That's the trouble with kids these days,' she complained, glaring at them from under her hair. 'No respect. Always rushing about, barging past you, never a please nor a thank-you. Wasn't like that when I was a gel. Jiw, no. Had a bit of respect in them days.'

Tati and Daio tried their best to imagine Gwrach y Rhibyn as a girl their age. It was impossible.

'We were just looking for Eldan,' Daio explained, very politely. 'You don't happen to have seen him around, do you?'

'No, I haven't,' the witch snapped. 'Don't want to, neither. Elves!' she added bitterly. 'Ought to be a law. Keeping respectable people awake all hours with that rock music. Good riddance, that's what I say. Is your Naino in?'

Tati blinked in surprise. 'Uh ... yes, I think so.'

'I'm just going up there to borrow a cup of sugar. Elves, indeed ...'

And away she went, crawling and snuffling, still muttering about *elves*.

'That's one visitor Naino could do without,' said Daio under his breath, when he was sure she was far enough away not to hear him.

'Naino can handle her,' said Tati confidently. 'C'mon.'

5

Humans

Half an hour later Tati and Daio were sitting in the topmost fork of a beech tree and looking doleful.

'I don't believe this,' Daio said gloomily. '*Everybody's* busy tonight. Nobody wants to talk to us, or have fun, or anything.'

'Miserable lot,' said Tati. 'And it's such a perfect night, too.'

It was. There was a huge bright harvest moon shining golden overhead, the air was almost as warm as summer, but mixed in with the drowsy scents of buddleia and late meadowsweet and fresh grass there was the darker, sharper smell of leaf mould. Autumn was on its way. It was a night for exploring and having adventures; for excitement and mischief and fun. Eldan would have been the perfect companion on a night like this – but Eldan had gone away.

Tati gazed at the little twinkling lights of the estate on the hill, and past them, lower down, at the harsh yellow glare of the sodium lights in Nant-y-Ceirw New Town. And into her head came an idea so new and so daring it took her breath away.

'Humans play,' she said.

Daio stared at her. 'But they can't see us! And anyway, we're not *allowed*!'

The Rules were very strict on this point. A bit of mischief now and again, perhaps (even the Rules had to admit that you can't expect bwganod to keep out of mischief) – but otherwise: NO DEALINGS WITH HUMANS. Humans were dangerous, dirty and not to be trusted, the grown-ups said.

Tati shrugged. 'Okay, forget it. Just an idea, that's all.'

But Daio was thinking it over, and his eyes began to sparkle.

'We could go and see where they live,' he suggested. 'It wouldn't do any harm, would it – just *looking*?'

They'd never tried to explore the places where humans lived. Partly because there'd always been plenty to do and lots of friends around; partly because of the Rules, but mainly because nobody had ever thought of such a thing before.

'What about the fence?' There were iron railings all around the Old Ironworks, to try to stop people dumping their rubbish there. The bwganod had been warned about iron, of course. Iron was the most dangerous thing of all. If you touched it, you were trapped. You couldn't float away, or dissolve, or change shape or anything. You were stuck, and helpless. It was just as well for Tati and Daio that there wasn't much iron inside the Old Ironworks any more – everything had long ago rusted into ruin. And of course they had always kept well away from the wrecks of old cars and the broken fridges and the rest of the rubbish.

'We just fly over it,' said Daio. 'No problem.'

Tati began to grin. 'It's worth a try. Let's go!'

In a few minutes, they were looking down on the roofs of the estate.

At this time of night, all the streets were deserted. One or two cars raced by with a deafening noise and a gust of exhaust fumes which made the bwganod cough. But otherwise, all the humans were indoors.

The estate seemed very strange to Tati and Daio. The houses were like boxes, all almost exactly the same – and they were all quite dead.

'It's the stuff they're made of,' Tati guessed – and she was right. Wood and stone are natural things, and alive in their own slow, dreaming way, like the old farmhouses high up on the mountain above the Ceirw Valley. But bricks and tiles and concrete blocks are man-made and lifeless.

They could sense iron everywhere, and lots of other metals too – and this reminded them to be extra careful. As they flew along a street between rows of gardens Daio pulled a couple of tall, smooth sticks out of a flowerbed.

'If you want to touch something, poke it with this.'

'Good thinking,' Tati nodded.

Most of the gardens were lawns, with a few shrubs growing here and there. Bwganod have a special closeness with trees of all kinds, so Tati and Daio dropped down to say hello. But the shrubs were mostly foreign, and didn't want to talk.

'Either they don't understand what we're saying to them, or they've forgotten how,' said Daio.

'All that smoke and pollution and stuff, I expect,' said Tati.

Just then a lady walked up one of the driveways, pressed a little lighted button at the side of the door and made chimes sound: Cling-clong!

A moment later the door opened and she went inside.

'Are you thinking what I'm thinking?' said Tati, and Daio grinned.

Using their sticks, they poked all the lighted buttons on all the doors in the street, flying very fast from one house to the next. In a few moments every door in the whole street was wide open and people were walking into the road and asking each other what on earth was going on and arguing about who the culprits were. Tati and Daio watched the commotion with glee.

Feeling bolder now, they flew to the next street and cautiously peeped in at a lighted window. They knew about glass from talking to the old farmhouses: glass wasn't dangerous, it was just a barrier.

Four humans were sitting in the room. (It was Sally-Ann's house, but of course the bwganod didn't know that). They were all facing the same way, and all four were staring at something just below the level of the sill. Tati and Daio couldn't see what it was, but they could see the ghostly flickering reflections which the Thing cast over the rest of the room. The humans weren't talking much, just watching the Thing, and their faces looked blank and bored.

Tati flew up a bit higher. One of the human children glanced up for an instant, and gave Tati a nasty fright – but the next moment he'd looked away and was staring at the Thing again.

'They really *can't* see us, can they?' Daio marvelled. 'Is it weird, or what?'

Tati floated boldly to the middle of the big window and flapped her arms. 'Oi! You in there!' she yelled. 'Yoo-hoo! Anybody home?' And she turned herself into a gigantic toad.

Nobody moved, or so much as glanced in her direction.

The two bwganod began to have fun. They flew across the window, taking it in turns to change into the most horrific illusions they could think of. They made rude faces through the glass. They stuck their fingers into the corners of their mouths and crossed their eyes and waggled their tongues.

The humans just sat there, gazing straight at them with blank faces, and didn't see a thing.

28

Tati and Daio were laughing so much that they didn't hear a snuffling, scuffling noise in the bushes under the window. So when a deep gruff voice said 'HEY! WHO'S THERE? HEY!' very loudly indeed right beneath them, they nearly jumped out of their skins with fright.

'Butcher!' said Tati, when she'd recovered.

The dog peered short-sightedly at them, and sniffed suspiciously. Then he began to grin, and wag his tail.

'Oh, it's you. Hello there.'

Butcher was one of the dogs who came through the Old Ironworks each day on his walk. The bwganod knew him quite well.

'What on earth are you two doing here?' he asked curiously. 'Not your scene, really, I shouldn't have thought.'

'Just having a look round, that's all,' Daio explained.

'You don't mind, do you?' Tati asked politely.

Butcher looked quite pleased. 'Good grief, no. Nice to see a friendly face now and again. Tell you what,' he offered, 'I'll give you one of my exclusive conducted tours if you like. All sorts of interesting things to sniff at round here, if you know where to go. There's a particularly niffy dead rat I've been saving for a special occasion like this. We could go and roll in it, if you like.'

'No, thanks,' the bwganod said hastily.

Butcher looked quite offended. 'Oh, if that's how you feel about it … Suit yourselves. Just trying to be friendly, that's all.'

'It's really kind of you, Butcher,' Daio assured him. 'We do appreciate the offer, honestly. It's just that dead rats aren't really our thing, know what I mean?'

Tati was more interested in the weird flickering lights inside the humans' room.

'What are they looking at in there?'

'Oh, that thing!' Butcher didn't bother to hide his disgust. 'That's the telly. Dreadful thing. Can't see the point of it myself. Smells awful, and when you go too close your fur crackles. Nasty, noisy contraption. Sure you'd rather not have a sniff at that rat?'

'Positive,' Tati said firmly. 'Sorry, Butcher. Thanks anyway.'

The curtains were drawn across all the other windows in Mostyn Close. Tati and Daio peered through the gaps, upstairs and downstairs. They saw families washing up in kitchens. They saw older children arguing and doing homework and listening to radios and younger children getting ready for bed. And lots and lots of people watching the mysterious Telly that Butcher had told them about.

'I always thought humans were filthy,' Tati said in astonishment. 'But they're quite clean and tidy really, aren't they?'

Up to now all they'd known about humans had been the disgusting mess they left all over the Old Ironworks – the cans and bottles and sweet wrappings and old newspapers as well as the polystyrene trays from the takeaways, the black plastic bags of rotting garbage and other rubbish.

At the furthest end of the estate there was a row of houses without upstairs windows. Here, too, the rooms were all snugly curtained off from the glorious moonlight – except for the last one in the row, where the curtains were open, and light streamed out across the lawn.

The bwganod hovered outside, and looked in.

There was only one human inside the room: a very thin, wrinkly human with white hair sticking out from under the flat brown cap he wore. He was sitting in a big chair with a checked rug tucked around his knees. He had huge bony, knuckly hands which rested on his lap as though they were too big and too heavy for the rest of him. His eyes were closed: he was asleep.

'He must be ever so old!' Daio whispered in awe. Even Bwgantaid looked younger than that – and Bwgantaid would be eight hundred and sixty-four years old next birthday.

Then they saw what was standing in full view in the corner of the room – and immediately forgot everything else. For there, in a squarish brown box, was Tiw the barn owl. Tati and Daio gasped with shock.

The owl in the box took no notice of them. It bent down, preened its feathered toes – and then, to their utter astonishment, *it got smaller* until it was a white dot sitting on the branch of a tiny tree. Then it raised its wings and flew away ... *into* the box!

'Tiw!' Daio wailed, horrified. He grabbed Tati's arm. 'He's got Tiw in that box! We've got to *do* something!'

Tati had been worried, too, for a few startled moments – but now she thought she understood. 'Don't be silly, it's not *real*! – it's a magic box that shows pictures of things, like Eldan's mother's looking glass.'

'Oh,' said Daio.

There was another owl inside the box now – a huge brown one with eartufts and fierce yellow eyes. Other owls flew to and fro, talking to each other in foreign accents. Daio was utterly entranced.

'It's better than a magic glass,' he whispered to Tati.

Tati was a bit shocked. It seemed somehow disloyal, if not downright wicked, to say that anything humans made was better than Elves. 'Not bad, I suppose,' she admitted grudgingly.

'Not bad? It's brilliant. Wish we could hear better, though.'

He drifted up higher to see. 'Hey, there's a a little window open up here!' And before Tati could stop him, he'd evaporated through the gap and was inside the human's room. He made rude faces at her through the glass.

'Daio! No! Come back!'

31

Daio grinned, and settled himself on the floor in front of the magic box.

Tati gulped. It was bad enough to have sneaked out of the Ironworks without telling anybody where they were going – but what on earth would Mamibwgan and Dadibwgan say if Daio got himself stuck inside a human house? She'd just have to go in after him, and drag him out by force.

The window frame was a wooden one, and the metal bar which propped the little top light open was pushed well to one side. Tati dissolved herself and very carefully oozed through.

'Daio! What d'you think you're *doing*? We're not *allowed*!' Usually it was Daio who said things like that to her.

They both turned round sharply to stare at the old man. His wrinkled face was set in deep, grumpy folds, and his eyes were still closed.

'It's okay,' Daio said confidently. 'He can't see us or hear us. And we can see the owls much better from here.'

Tati wasn't happy. 'Well, all right – as long as we get out the *instant* he wakes up – understand?'

Inside the magic box owls were feeding their chicks and complaining that the cheeping and squawking was driving them round the bend. A human lady's voice was talking at the same time – but she didn't seem to understand what the owls themselves were saying.

'Can't she hear them, or something?' Tati asked, and Daio shrugged.

And then all of a sudden real, heavy human footsteps sounded just outside the sitting-room door.

The bwganod froze. Then Tati grabbed Daio and dragged him behind the sideboard. Perhaps humans really couldn't see bwganod – but in a situation like this Tati wasn't prepared to take the risk. She and Daio hovered very still

between the dusty wall and the even dustier wooden panels of the sideboard, and held their breath.

The sitting-room door opened, and a youngish woman came in. She was wearing a coat and carrying a shopping-bag.

'All right now, Gramps?' she said in a loud, too-cheerful voice. 'I'll just draw the curtains for you and then I'll be off home. Anything else you want before I go?'

The old man opened his eyes and looked sourer and grumpier than ever.

'You don't have to shout,' he told her. 'I can hear you quite well without shouting.'

The woman took no notice. She pulled the curtains across the big window (shutting the little top light as she did so), and picked up a cup and saucer from the table beside the old man's chair.

'See you tomorrow then – all right?'

'Aye, most likely,' the old man said.

'Good night, then, Gramps.'

'Good night, Susie.'

The woman shut the sitting-room door behind her. Tati and Daio heard faint clattering noises coming from somewhere, and the noise of running water. Then the footsteps tapped briskly down the hall, and the front door slammed. The footsteps went on down the concrete path outside and along the pavement until they faded away in the distance.

The old man lifted his head and glared round the room. Now that he was properly awake, the eyes under the heavy bushy eyebrows were extremely bright and sharp.

'I know you're there,' he said. 'Come out by here now, where I can see you.'

Tati and Daio went cold with horror. He'd known they were there all along!

'Come out, now,' he commanded in a stern voice. 'I haven't got all night.'

They looked round frantically for a way of escape. There wasn't one. They were trapped inside a human house with an old man who could actually *see* them ... a human who had a magic box and who might easily be a wizard, or even worse ...

It was a bad moment.

Very slowly they oozed out from behind the sideboard and hovered nervously in front of him. They dared not dissolve, or change shape, just in case he did have magical powers they didn't know about. Nasty things can happen to a bwgan if magic catches you between shapes.

The old man looked them up and down. It was hard to tell from his expression whether he was surprised at what he saw, or disappointed.

'You're not very big, are you?' he said at last.

'We will be big, one day,' said Daio indignantly.

'We're bwganod,' said Tati.

34

The grumpy old face began to soften into the beginnings of a smile. 'Oh, I can see that,' he said. Then he scowled ferociously. 'So what in the name of Goodness are the pair of you doing in here? Haunting a rubbishy new bungalow that's only been up five minutes?'

He sounded so like Bwgantaid in one of his moods that suddenly Tati found she wasn't afraid of him any more. And when you looked closely you could see that his eyes were twinkling under the eyebrows, even though the rest of his face was scowling.

'We're not *haunting*!' she said. 'Bwganod don't haunt places!'

'We came to see the magic box,' Daio explained.

'Magic box? What magic box?'

Tati pointed. The owls were flying into the sunset, and human writing was rising up the glass front, in rows. The bwganod couldn't read the words.

Gramps was really smiling now. 'That's not a magic box, boys bach, that's a telly.'

'It's magic to us,' said Tati.

A human face had appeared in the box, and was talking.

'Can we see the owls again, please?' Daio begged.

It turned out that they couldn't. 'You need a video for that,' Gramps said.

They didn't ask him what a video was; they had a nasty feeling that even if he did try to explain, they wouldn't understand. The things humans surrounded themselves with seemed to be dreadfully complicated.

Instead, they pressed all the buttons on Gramps's magic stick, and watched the pictures change one after another until he complained of feeling giddy. The stick itself was a big surprise – it kept slipping and slithering through their fingers as though it was made of ice.

'Plastic,' said Gramps, nodding wisely to himself, and

found them a piece of wood to poke the buttons with instead.

They had the same problem when he took them into the kitchen to fetch some fizzy lemonade from the fridge.

'Hold that a minute, will you?' Gramps said, thrusting a white plastic box into Tati's hands while he bent down creakily to rummage inside the fridge. Tati did her best to hold on, but she couldn't. The box shot out from between her fingers, skidded across the worktop and knocked a bottle of milk and a tray of eggs onto the floor. Tati was horrified.

'Oh, don't you worry about a little thing like that,' Gramps told her comfortingly. 'Her 'cross the road'll clean it up in the morning.'

They didn't like the kitchen much. It was full of dangerous metal; they couldn't cope with the plastic containers; and worst of all, they both began to itch and sneeze.

'Synthetics,' said Gramps. 'Always knew they was rubbish. You go back in the sitting-room where there's a good, honest-to-God wool carpet, and I'll bring you the pop now.'

Back in the sitting-room, Tati and Daio sipped fizzy lemonade out of two little pottery bowls with *A Present from Betws-y-Coed* written in curly letters on the sides, and nibbled chocolate biscuits out of a paper packet. Human food was a bit weird, they decided, but nice. Between mouthfuls of biscuit they told Gramps all about themselves, and about Mamibwgan and Dadibwgan and Bwganbabi and Naino and Taid and the Bwganhouse, and all their other friends amongst the People of the Wood. And Gramps listened and asked questions and laughed out loud and began to look years younger and much happier than when they'd first seen him.

Then he told them how he'd got to know about bwganod.

Once, long ago, when he'd been young, he'd seen a bwgan lady in the Ceirw woods.

'Beautiful, she was. Long hair down to her knees, and flowers on her head like a crown. Didn't see me, though. I was afraid to breathe, in case I scared her away.'

'Sounds like Mami,' Tati said.

'Aye. Wouldn't surprise me. Got a look of her about the pair of you. Specially you,' he added, glaring at Tati.

They were used to his grumpy ways by now, and weren't put off.

'I thought you said the lady was pretty,' Daio objected. 'Tati's not pretty.'

'You shut your mouth, boyo,' Gramps told him crossly. 'Beautiful, I said. Different thing altogether. And that's how your sister's going to be one of these days, you watch.'

Tati blinked, and tried not to show how pleased she felt. She knew she wasn't pretty, and it had never worried her in the slightest. In her opinion, pretty girls were a pain. But it was nice to hear somebody say that one day she'd be as beautiful as Mami. It gave her a warm, glowing feeling inside.

Then Gramps told them a bit about himself. How he'd been a coal miner for years and years, working in the stifling dark, underground. He showed them his hands, which were covered all over with little blue marks where he'd been cut and scratched by the coal.

'Won't wash out,' he explained. 'They're with me for good now. That's where I got this bad chest, see. Pneumoconiosis. Seventy per cent dust, I got. Can't catch my breath, some days. That's why I'm stuck in here on my own and can't get out and about no more.'

Tati and Daio were appalled. It seemed such a dreadful way to have lived.

'Oh, no,' Gramps said. 'We had our good times and our bad times, like everybody else.'

Time had passed very quickly, and it was a lot later than any of them had realised. So they all got a nasty shock when they heard the sound of a key being turned in the front door.

'It's that nurse,' Gramps said, 'come to help me get to bed. Off you go now, quick sharp.'

He opened the window wide, and they wafted through just in time to hear the sitting-room door open and a scolding voice say, 'Honestly, Mr Evans, you'll catch your death with the window wide open like that. And what's all this mess in the kitchen?'

They didn't wait to hear Gramps's reply, but headed straight for home. Daio was feeling a bit peculiar after all the fizzy lemonade. Every time he burped, he shot two metres up into the air.

'We could go and see him again,' Tati suggested.

'He wants us to,' Daio agreed.

As they flew over the wood, Tati got rather thoughtful. 'I don't think we ought to tell anybody about him, though. Not straight away.'

'Why? Was it bad, what we did?'

'No, not exactly, but ...' Tati was struggling with her conscience. If Mami and Dadi found out where they'd been, they'd have to put a stop to any more visits. Rules were Rules, after all, and not there to be broken whenever you felt like it.

On the other hand, Gramps was so lonely. He'd enjoyed their company, you could tell, and he'd be terribly disappointed if he never saw them again.

What do you do in a situation like that?

'We didn't do any harm, though, did we?' said Daio.

'I spilt some milk and broke some eggs,' said Tati glumly.

'Yeah, but apart from that, it was okay.'

'Tell you what,' said Tati. 'If they ask where we've been, we'll tell them. But if they don't ask ...'

'Anyway,' said Daio, 'the Rules don't say we shouldn't *watch* humans, do they?'

And with that thought easing their guilty consciences, they flew home.

6

Bethan's Birthday

For Tati and Daio, home was their Bwganhouse. They couldn't imagine having to live anywhere else.

The Bwganhouse grew in a little green glade in the wildest part of the Ceirw Valley. On the outside all you could see of it was a small thicket of young oak trees, with their shiny, silky grey stems packed tightly together. There was a door, if you knew exactly where and how to look for it, and leaf-shaped windows like the filigree spaces between winter twigs. But the whole clump was so small – not much bigger than the average dustbin, in fact – that it was hard to understand how an entire family of medium-to-large bwganod could possibly fit inside it.

That was where the magic came in.

The inside of the Bwganhouse was bigger than its outside – in fact, it could be as big as it needed to be at any time. The walls were living leaves, which never got tired-looking and never turned brown; and the slender young branches interlaced overhead to make a snug, dry roof. The floor was clean green grass, and in the middle of the big round living-room stood a bowl of Mami's magic stones which shone forever with a clear golden light. The stones provided heat for cooking and for warming the Bwganhouse in winter.

In the wall were leafy arches leading to the other rooms. There were two small rooms for Tati and Daio, an even smaller one for Bwganbabi, and lastly the big sunlit room which belonged to Mamibwgan and Dadibwgan.

Bwganod don't need much sleep, so when they were tired Tati and Daio just dozed in their cradles of woven leaves while the Bwganhouse crooned songs to them, or told them stories. The Bwganhouse, being magical, was a lot more than just a home, or a shelter from the weather. It was a living being, with a personality of its own, a member of the bwgan family as important as Mami or Dadi.

They all loved the Bwganhouse dearly, and it loved and cared for them in return.

Because they'd always lived there, Tati and Daio had tended to take the Bwganhouse a bit for granted, and it wasn't until they started visiting Gramps in his bungalow on the estate that they'd begun to realise just how special the Bwganhouse was, and how lucky they were.

'Wouldn't it be nice if Gramps could come to our house?' said Daio.

But that, they knew, was absolutely out of the question. Even if the Rules had permitted it (which they didn't), Gramps couldn't possibly have walked that far. Even going into the kitchen to fetch their lemonade had made him breathless, and wobbly at the knees.

They'd been to see him quite a few times since that first visit – but they still hadn't told Mami or Dadi or the Bwganhouse about him. To be fair, they had tried, once or twice, to steer the conversation round to the subject of humans – but each time something had happened to interrupt them before they'd got as far as mentioning Gramps. Just now, Mami and Dadi had more important things to think about. Autumn is a busy time for bwganod: Winter is approaching, and all the trees need their help in settling down for their long winter sleep.

'One day soon we'll tell them everything,' Tati and Daio kept promising. And in the meantime, because they really couldn't see any harm in what they were doing, they explored the whole estate and even ventured along the main road as far as Nant-y-Ceirw High Street.

It was the coldest morning so far that term. The first frosts had come early that year. Everywhere, the leaves were turning golden on the trees and falling in great drifts on paths and in gardens. As Eleri and Bethan and Sally-Ann walked up the little back lane to school, the grass and the hedges were furry with glittering white frost and the frozen mud scrunched under their feet.

Lots of people used the little back lane in the mornings. If you came to school by car, it was convenient for parents because the entrance was on a through road: they could park easily and then drive away. The main school entrance was in a cul-de-sac and between eight-thirty and nine o'clock it was jammed solid with buses and cars and scurrying children and harassed grown-ups trying to do three-point turns where there wasn't enough space. It was not a good place to end up in if you were a parent in a hurry to get to work.

All three girls were wearing their warm winter coats. Eleri and Sally-Ann had mittens and woolly caps. Bethan had a pale blue fluffy hand-muff slung on a blue silk cord round her neck, and ear-muffs to match: a birthday present from her cousins in Canada. Eleri and Sally-Ann thought she looked very smart.

And inside the muff, cradled cosily between Bethan's warm, plump hands, was another birthday present: her brand-new Sammie doll, with two new outfits, which she'd brought to show the other girls at dinner time.

As they trudged up the lane the three girls were chattering like parakeets: about Bethan's birthday party, which was tonight, after school; about Bonfire Night, which was only three weeks away; and of course about Christmas which wasn't for another two months but getting closer all the time. They were talking so much they slowed down without realising it. All the other children pushed past them and by the time they'd reached the gate leading into the school field, everybody else had already gone round to the front yard to wait for the bell. The field was empty.

'We'll be late!' said Eleri anxiously.

But just as she was pushing the gate open, four very large and solid shapes rose out of the bushes alongside.

'Hello-ello-ello,' one of them said in a loud, jeering voice – and the three girls went cold with sudden fright.

'The big boys,' Eleri whispered. 'Oh, no ...'

The boys were from the Big School on the other side of the town – and they were bullies. Just recently they'd started hanging about outside the Primary School and making a nuisance of themselves. They appeared at play-times and dinner times, and even before school started in the mornings. They joined in football games and spoilt everybody's fun by being rough and clumsy on purpose, and knocking the smaller boys over into the mud. Once they'd even broken a window by kicking the ball too hard, and the Primary School boys had got the blame. Only last week, they'd stolen Warren's new football and he'd had to start saving up his pocket money all over again to buy another one.

The teachers and the dinner ladies shooed them away whenever they saw them. But teachers and dinner ladies can't be everywhere at once, and the big boys were experts at keeping out of their way.

It wasn't only the boys they bullied, it was the girls too. They teased people, and pulled people's hair, and stole things. Only two days ago they'd run off with Sally-Ann's roller skates – and Sally-Ann had got into bad trouble at home when her mother had found out they were missing.

All the children were scared of the big boys. But nobody dared tell the grown-ups what was going on. The big boys threatened to do awful things to you if you did tell – and they were so big and so strong that you had to believe them.

The leader of the gang was called Brynmor Williams, and he was evil.

Now all four boys stood in a circle round Eleri and Bethan and Sally-Ann. The boys were grinning and swaggering a bit, and chewing gum like the baddies in Westerns. The girls shrank close together, quaking with fright.

'What have you got there, then?' Brynmor said to Bethan.

'N-nothing,' Bethan stammered, and tried to hide her new muff under her coat.

'Aw, c'mon, gi's a look, then,' another boy said, sniggering. His hand shot out and wrenched the muff away. The cord broke, hurting Bethan's neck – and the next moment the gang was playing catch with her birthday present. As they hurled the muff over the girls' heads (too high and too fast for them to catch it, however high they tried to jump) Bethan's new doll fell out.

One of the boys pounced on it, and held it up.

'You leave that alone,' Sally-Ann yelled. 'That's Bethan's new doll!'

'Oh, it's a doll, is it?' Brynmor said, pretending to be astonished. 'Well, well, fancy that. And I thought it was a football!' And just to prove his point, he stuck the doll's head into the mud where the frost had thawed, and kicked it hard. The head broke off. Bethan began to cry. The doll's body went sailing into the air, and the other boys chased it, laughing in that nasty snuffling way big boys do.

'Stop it! Stop it!' Eleri shrieked. 'Give it back!'

'I'll tell my dad on you!' Bethan sobbed.

Brynmor leaned down very close and grabbed a handful of Bethan's hair. He twisted it until she yelped with pain.

'Now you listen to me. You tell on us, and I'll bring my gang round to your house in the middle of the night and we'll smash the whole place to smithereens. Understand?'

'Ye-ye-yes,' Bethan gasped.

Just then the bell went, and the four boys ran off.

Bethan was almost too scared to go home after school that day. Her muff was muddy and torn and so were the lovely new outfits for the doll. Sammie herself, of course, was broken beyond repair. The row she had from her mother was worse than Sally-Ann's row over the missing roller skates. And it was her birthday, too.

'I can't understand it,' Bethan's mother said angrily. 'I always thought Eleri and Sally-Ann were nice sensible girls – but every time you've played with them at school recently you've come home filthy dirty and with your toys broken.'

Sally-Ann's mother had said much the same sort of thing to Sally-Ann about Bethan and Eleri. The birthday party was a dismal failure because none of the mothers were speaking to each other. A big row was building up between the families of the Mostyn Close children.

The girls remembered what Brynmor had said, and were too frightened to tell anybody what had really happened.

Next morning the swings which the PTA had bought for the nursery class were tied up in knots, and their seats smashed.

'Vandals,' the caretaker said angrily – but nobody thought to connect the incident of the broken swings with Sally-Ann's missing skates and Warren's lost football and Bethan's doll. The children all guessed, of course – but they weren't saying anything.

7

Paints, Chalks and Dustbins

A few days later Tati and Daio were sitting in a tree in Mostyn Close and watching five children climb out of five separate cars with their school bags. The children didn't even try to talk to one another. They just scuttled up the drives of their own houses as fast as they could.

Tati and Daio didn't know about the rows, of course, or about the bullies. They were on their way home after visiting Gramps.

'Where do they go all day?' Tati wondered.

'I asked Gramps that,' Daio said. 'He said School.'

'School? What's that?'

Tati and Daio had regular lessons with Mamibwgan, of course, and lessons with the Elves whenever they happened to be around. But nobody had ever mentioned the word school before.

'You don't want to know,' said a mournful voice below them. 'Believe me, you'd definitely rather not know.'

'Hello, Butcher,' said Tati cheerfully. She and Daio floated down for a chat.

Daio was curious. 'Why? What's wrong with it?'

Butcher blew through his whiskers in a disgusted snort. 'Absolutely pointless, that's what's wrong with it. Went there once, you know. When I was a lot younger, of course. Just a puppy, actually. Enthusiastic, inquisitive, that sort of thing.' To the bwganod's surprise, Butcher had gone quite pink around the nose.

'So, what do they do there?'

Butcher's nose got even pinker. 'Actually, the fact is, I followed them. All the way there. Most embarrassing.'

'Why embarrassing?'

Butcher shuddered. 'Well ... you know what puppies are like. Jumping up, barking, having little ... er ... accidents ... I wouldn't do it *now*, of course,' he added virtuously. 'We older residents have a – how shall I put it? – a certain dignity to maintain.' He looked round to see if anybody else was listening. 'By the way, I'd appreciate it if you kept that little incident to yourselves, if you don't mind. I wouldn't like it to get around. Street cred, and all that, you know.' Like many people, Butcher was much more interested in telling you how he'd felt about something than in describing what had actually happened.

'Yes, fine, no problem – but what was it *like*, Butcher?'

'What?'

Tati was running out of patience. 'The school place. What do they do there? What's it like inside?'

'Oh, the *school* ... Well, you can't run about much, for a start. You have to sit down on chairs, and talk quietly, and make marks on paper with little sticks with hairs on the end ...'

Daio's ears pricked up. '*Painting*?' His eyes shone. He loved painting.

'Oh, is that what you call it? Didn't think much of it myself, mind,' Butcher said disparagingly. 'Smells awful, tastes worse. In fact the whole place smells terrible. I wouldn't go there if I were you.'

'Sounds okay to me,' Daio remarked, remembering the dead rat.

Butcher looked a bit put out. 'Oh, well,' he said huffily, 'don't say I didn't warn you.'

He turned his back on them and waddled importantly away up the Close, looking the very image of middle-aged doggy respectability.

At that precise moment a large black cat jumped down from a wall and crossed the road in front of him.

Butcher's eyes weren't very good, and he didn't see the cat until she was quite close. His head jerked up, his tail stiffened – and the next instant he'd forgotten all about being dignified and respectable. Barking joyously, ears flapping and tail streaming, he galloped off in pursuit.

Unfortunately, Butcher was a bit overweight (and definitely under-fit) – and as he ran the bits of him that weren't galloping wobbled about and got in the way of the bits that were. Meanwhile the cat was doing its thousand-legs-a-second impression without actually moving very fast (an unnerving habit cats have, especially when crossing the road in front of cars) – and for a few moments it almost looked as though Butcher was going to catch up.

But the cat knew exactly what she was doing. She let Butcher get within half a metre of her tail – and then she put on a terrific burst of speed and vanished up a tree.

Butcher didn't see the tree until it was too late to swerve. He put on all four brakes hard, skidded the last few metres on his ample bottom and came to a stop with his nose a whisker away from the trunk. The cat made sarcastic remarks at him from the branch above his head.

Tati and Daio were laughing so much they nearly fell out of the bush they were in. It was mean of them, but they couldn't help it – Butcher had looked so funny.

Butcher himself was utterly mortified. He picked himself up, shook himself all over, glanced round furtively to see if anybody besides the bwganod had been watching, and then stalked away very deliberately with his nose in the air as if to say, 'Who, *me*? No, I *never* chase cats. Whoever you saw just then, it couldn't have been *me*!'

'C'mon,' Tati said. 'Let's go home.'

They flew off up the Ceirw Valley to the Bwganhouse.

When they got there, however, they found the Bwgan-house packed to bursting-point with visitors, and as noisy as a starling roost. All the bwgan-aunts had arrived to spend the evening with Mami.

Mamibwgan and her eleven sisters hadn't seen each other for months, and there seemed to be an enormous amount of gossip to catch up on, and lots to laugh about. All twelve sisters were talking at once, and the noise was unbelievable. The Bwganhouse itself was quivering all over with excitement and hospitality and delight.

'Where's Dadi?' asked Daio.

Dadi had stayed and been polite for half an hour or so, then he'd discovered something terribly important to do at the furthest end of the Ceirw Valley and had escaped, leaving the sisters to their fun and chatter.

Tati and Daio were roped in to pass round honey cakes and cowslip wine. Just as they were beginning to get bored (they didn't know the people the aunts were talking about, and didn't understand any of the jokes) Mamibwgan said gently, 'Why don't you two just float away and amuse yourselves for a while? You don't really want to listen to all this grown-up gossip, do you?' – and, thankfully, they too made their escape.

Outside in the wood the frost was glittering like fallen starlight under the moon.

'I *do* like them,' Tati said. 'They're really fantastic Aunts – one at a time!'

'I know. But when they all get together like that ...'

'Dadi had the right idea, disappearing the minute they arrived.'

'He stayed for a bit,' Daio said, defending him. 'He likes them too – in small doses!'

'What I can't understand,' Tati said thoughtfully, 'is how he ever managed to get Mami on her own for long enough to decide he wanted to marry her.'

They floated idly over the Old Ironworks.

'What'll we do now?' Tati said. 'We could go and find Dadi, or go and see Gramps again. Or we could go and have a look at this school place. What d'you reckon?'

Daio knew exactly what he wanted to do.

'I want to see those paints.'

'Better find Butcher, then,' said Tati.

Butcher was snuffling round his garden in Mostyn Close.

'Walkies, Butcher!' Tati called.

'Oh, I say!' said Butcher excitedly, and began to bark and jump about. Suddenly his expression changed, and he stopped.

'Hang on a minute. What am I *doing*? I can't go on a you-know-what with you two!'

'Why not?'

'*Why not*? Because self-respecting dogs don't go on W-A-L-K-S with bwganod, that's why not. I'd never live it down.'

'You mean walkies?' Tati said wickedly.

Instantly Butcher began to jump about and bark. He controlled himself with a big effort.

'Don't *say* that word!' he pleaded. 'I can't help myself, and it's most embarrassing. It's what they call a conditioned reflex.'

Daio put on his best wheedling voice. 'Oh, come on, Butcher, don't be a spoilsport. Nobody'll notice, and it's a lovely night for a you-know-what.'

Butcher wasn't completely stupid. He said suspiciously, 'Where exactly d'you want me to take you?'

'The school,' said Daio.

'What, all that way?'

'You managed it when you were a puppy,' Tati said reasonably. 'It can't be all that far. Please, Butcher. You're the only one who knows where it is.'

In fact, the school was further than they'd thought. Because Butcher was with them, they had to follow the main road, with its shops and bright yellow lights and smelly, snarling cars. At first Butcher trotted along with his tail tucked well down, muttering things like, 'If anyone I know sees me with you two, I shall never live it down, never,' and 'You do realise, don't you, that I could be arrested for this, and put in the dog pound?'

After a while, however, the exercise cheered him up and he began to give them interesting doggy bits of information about the places they were passing.

'My namesake,' he said importantly, sniffing at a shop which had hunks of meat in the window. 'Charming fellow. Great friend of mine.'

The school and the playing fields were like an island of darkness in the middle of the brightly-lit housing estate. Even Mr Johnson the caretaker had gone home, and everywhere was deserted.

Bwganod, as you know, can see in the dark. Tati and Daio peered through the big plate glass windows. They saw small wooden tables and chairs, brightly painted in different colours, and rows of books on shelves, and the children's paintings on the walls.

'How do we get in?' Daio asked eagerly.

Butcher didn't know, and wasn't interested in finding out. 'If you don't mind,' he said, 'I think I'll just go and sniff round the dustbins for a bit. Give me a shout when you're ready to go home.'

Tati came flying excitedly round the corner of the building. 'There's a window open. Like Gramps's, only smaller.'

At the back of the school part of the hill had been cut away to make room for a little yard where the dustbins were. A little further along, there was a small window with the top light open.

Luckily for the bwganod, the window frame was a wooden one again. If it had been metal, they wouldn't have stood a chance of getting inside. As it was, however, they dissolved themselves and oozed through.

They found themselves in a cloakroom, with white china washbasins all along one wall, and a long bench opposite with rows of iron pegs above it. The only things hanging on the pegs were somebody's scarf, and a rather dusty mitten that Mr. Johnson had found behind one of the radiators.

The sight of so much iron was frightening – so the bwganod floated quickly through the open door and began to explore the classrooms.

They found the art room almost at once. On a table, in plain view, were the children's paints, all set out ready for tomorrow's lessons. They were in flat cakes of bright colours in little plastic trays, and beside them stood a jar full of wooden-handled brushes. In a sink nearby there was even a jam jar full of clean water, and on another table was a neat stack of painting paper.

Daio's eyes shone. He'd done a lot of painting, mostly with Elf-paints, which are pastes in pots – and he was very good at it. It wasn't hard to work out how to use these strange-smelling human paints.

'But for heaven's sake don't touch the iron bit on the brush,' Tati warned.

While Daio was experimenting, Tati wandered round the room looking at the pictures the children had painted. She could appreciate the houses and the humans and the cars – they all looked fine – but the trees seemed most peculiar.

'What on earth's this?' she said, pointing to a picture of something with a chocolate-brown stem and a bright green fuzz like a mop on top. 'I've never seen a tree like that in my life!'

'One of those foreign palm things?' Daio suggested.

Tati wrinkled her forehead. 'Maybe.' Then she had a disturbing thought. 'Perhaps they can't *see* trees like we do.'

Daio snorted. 'If you ask me, they don't really *look* at anything much. Tell you what – I'll paint them a *real* tree.'

They argued a bit about which of their many tree-friends Daio should paint.

'Derwen's nice. Or Gwern.'

'Gwern's a bit complicated,' Daio said. 'All those fiddly little cones and things. No – I'll paint Esyllt as she is now, in the Autumn.'

Esyllt was a silver birch tree who grew in an old quarry just below the Bwganhouse. She was a very beautiful young tree, and one of their best friends.

While Daio was painting, Tati poked about and found some chalks in a tray beside the blackboard. Chalks are natural things, and once Tati had found this out she began to fill the blackboard with poems and stories in Elf-writing. Quite soon the blackboard was full, so she wrote on the walls on each side.

Daio's painting of Esyllt was coming along beautifully. He painted with his eyes half shut so that he could see her better in his mind. He painted her leaves like a shower of gold, and her silver trunk with the black streaks on it, and her roots going down into the soil amongst the stones and the rabbit-burrows and the earthworms.

They were both so engrossed that they didn't hear Butcher's warning bark. What they did hear – very suddenly, and alarmingly close – was the crash of breaking glass.

Tati and Daio froze.

There was another crash, and the clinking sound of glass fragments falling; then a lot of snuffling, low-voiced human laughter. The door of the art room was pushed open and three large boys burst in. They were followed by a fourth, who was sucking his finger and complaining.

'I cut my hand on that glass, I did.'

'Aw, shut up, you,' said the biggest boy.

'It's bleeding – look!'

'I said shut up, didn't I?'

The biggest boy looked round the room, which was faintly lit by the distant street lamps.

'Right. This room first, okay? Everything into the middle. Who's got the spray cans?'

'Me,' said the next biggest.

'Well, don't hang about, get a move on. Gwynfor, you go next door and start there.'

And to the bwganod's horror the boys began to overturn the tables and smash the chairs and rip down the curtains and the pictures, and tip the books off the shelves. Then they piled everything up in the middle of the floor. Crash!

54

went the table where Daio had been painting, and into the pile went all the paints and brushes. Daio's picture of Esyllt was torn away from under his nose and crumpled up with the rest.

'Stop it! What d'you think you're *doing*? Stop it!' Daio yelled – and dashed in amongst the boys. But they couldn't hear him, and they were so much bigger than he was that they couldn't even feel his kicks and punches. Meanwhile, the boy with the spray can was spraying paint all over the walls and the ceiling.

Butcher appeared at the window, barking furiously. Tati shouted to him through the glass.

'Butcher! Do something! Fetch the other dogs!'

'On my way,' Butcher barked. 'Get the nee-naw car,' he told her.

'The what?'

'The one with the flashing lights that goes nee-naw, nee-naw. It'll stop them. That's what it's for.'

'But how?'

'Use the phone, dimwit,' said Butcher, and dashed off.

'Phone,' thought Tati, and gulped. Gramps had a phone, and he'd told her all about the police. You pressed the nine button three times and told the police where to come. But she was a bwgan. The humans inside the phone wouldn't be able to hear her.

And now one of the boys was bending down and striking a match. A corner of one of the papers in the pile caught fire, and flames began to curl and spread.

Miraculously, there was still some water in the jar. Daio picked it up, dodged under the boy's arm and poured water on the flames. They sputtered and went out. Then he hit the boy with the jam jar, hard.

The boy backed away, clutching his bleeding nose and staring in horror at the jar which had floated around all by itself.

'D-did you see that? It hit me!'

That was when Tati had her brilliant idea. She grabbed Daio's arm just as he was bracing himself for another punch.

'No! Not that way! Frighten them instead!'

Leaving Daio to throw things, Tati looked round frantically for something to cover herself with – something not too heavy (which ruled out the curtains). In a little room just across the hall she found a small bed covered with a clean white sheet. She draped herself in it and glided back into the art room.

'Wh-what's that?' said the boy who'd hurt his finger. Tati waved her arms slowly up and down, and began to float towards him. He gave a screech.

'It's a ghost! It's a ghost!'

All the boys had seen Tati by now – a pale, eerie figure drifting soundlessly round the dimly-lit room. She swooped threateningly over their heads, and they cowered in terror.

'B-b-blimey,' Brynmor whimpered. 'Let's get out of here!'

They made a rush for the door, but Tati got there first. Then books and rulers and jars of paint began flying at the boys from all directions. One of the painting easels started walking round the room all by itself. Sobbing with fright, the big boys backed into a corner, ducking and squealing as things hit them on the head.

One of the books Daio threw hit a light switch. Instantly one of the overhead lights flickered on, nearly blinding everybody with its harsh white glare.

'That's it! Keep doing that! On and off, all over the school,' Tati shouted gleefully. 'I'll keep them penned up here! And see if you can find a phone!'

Surely somebody on the estate would notice if the lights kept flashing on and off?

The trouble with putting the light on was that now the

boys could see that the Thing which had frightened them so much was nothing but an empty sheet. Perhaps there *was* a ghost inside it – but if so, it was a very small one. And anyway, everybody is a lot braver with the lights on.

Suddenly the boys charged, yelling. They hurled Tati against the wall and burst out into the room with the broken window. And stopped, flabbergasted.

Into the school yard hundreds of dogs were pouring, with Butcher in the lead. Big dogs, little dogs, Alsatians and Labradors and golden retrievers and terriers and collies and poodles and spaniels – all the dogs from all the estates for miles around, come in response to Butcher's barked SOS because the bwganod needed their help. They leapt through the broken window and hurled themselves joyfully at the boys, growling and snarling and snapping their teeth.

The boys retreated into the art room again and slammed the door. They would have tried to break a window there but for the line of dogs keeping guard outside.

'Where's the phone?' Tati yelled.

'In the little room next to where you got the sheet.'

Lights were flashing on and off all over the school. Daio was punching the switches with a broom handle.

The lady at the telephone exchange got through to the police station.

'I'm getting 999 calls one after another, but nobody's answering. The call's coming from the school.'

Meanwhile the people on the estate had begun to notice the lights, and to call the police themselves. Mr Johnson arrived, took one look at what was happening and drove straight down to the police station to report in person. Soon, to Butcher's delight, the police cars started to arrive, with their own flashing lights and sirens blaring. They screeched to a halt in the playground.

'The cops!' wailed the boys. But it was too late: uniformed policemen were already running across the yard, with Mr Johnson amongst them, waving his bunch of keys.

The boys made a last, desperate attempt to break through the pack of dogs. Brynmor, being the biggest, was the only one who managed to scramble out of the broken window: the rest were held by eager teeth until the police came.

Brynmor headed for the high, steep bank behind the dustbins, with Butcher in hot pursuit. Using the bins as a launching pad, Brynmor jumped and grabbed the top of the wall, kicking Butcher viciously as he scrambled to the top. Above the wall, the bank was a slope of earth with tussocks of grass. He was nearly at the top when his foot caught on one of Sally-Ann's roller skates which were stuck there, wheels uppermost, in the soft earth. The wheels spun, his foot shot out from under him, and he began to slide back down the bank. He clawed frantically at the grass clumps, which pulled away in his hands, and then he fell, landing with a clanging, clattering crash amongst the bins and the garbage. Butcher himself stood guard over him, growling ferociously, until a policeman arrived to take the big boy away.

Next morning the teachers and the police inspected the damage. Everybody else had been sent home as soon as they'd arrived.

'It could have been a lot worse,' the Headmaster said sadly. 'There's still the broken window, and the smashed furniture, and the graffiti on the walls ... but if that fire had taken hold, we would have lost the whole school.'

'We got them all, anyway,' the policeman said. 'Nasty little bunch of bullies. Been hanging round the school for some time, I gather.'

The policeman had been talking to some of the children and their parents. Now that Brynmor and his gang had been caught, the whole story of the bullying had been coming out bit by bit.

'Bullying is the one thing I can't stand,' said the Head-master. 'But if the children are too frightened to tell you about it, what can you do?'

'What I don't understand,' said the policeman, 'is what all those dogs were doing here. And why were all the lights flashing on and off? And who was making those 999 calls? It's as though somebody was trying to warn us. It wasn't any of the boys. So who was it? The whole thing's a mystery, if you ask me.'

Later that day, the teachers started clearing up the mess in the art room. They looked wonderingly at Tati's writing on the blackboard.

'Weird,' one of them said. 'It looks like writing ... but I've never seen a script like that before.'

'Whatever it is, it's beautifully done,' another teacher said.

The third teacher found Daio's crumpled painting, and smoothed it out for them all to see. 'Look at this! Whoever painted this is a genius! How many children do you know who see trees in this way?'

'It's a complete mystery,' the first teacher sighed. 'None of those boys showed any interest in art or writing or anything else when they were at this school. But if it wasn't them – then who was it?'

'Pity about the painting,' Tati had said to Daio as they'd made their way back to the Bwganhouse.

Daio shrugged. 'Oh, well. Perhaps I'll do another one for them some time. A great big huge one, right across one wall.'

'That'll show 'em,' Tati chuckled gleefully.

'Won't it just,' said Daio smugly.

8

Life is Complicated

Gramps was in hospital, having a check-up. Tati and Daio discovered this when they called at his bungalow one evening and found him packing pyjamas and shaving things into a little suitcase.

'Her 'cross the road got it down for me this morning. Wanted to pack it for me as well. No, I said. I can do my own packing, thank you very much. I'm not mental yet, I told her straight.' He didn't like the lady who came in to clean.

Although he was much too proud and stubborn to say so, he was actually very glad of the bwganod's help. The effort of fetching what he wanted from the bathroom and the airing cupboard had made him breathless.

'What's a hospital?' said Daio.

Gramps looked even sourer and grumpier than before. 'Miserable old place,' he said, 'where they put no-hopers like me when they want to get rid of them for good.'

Tati was frightened. '*What?* L-like a *prison*, or something? Like an *iron cage*?'

Gramps saw straight away that he'd said something very silly.

'Don't be so daft, gel. Take no notice of a grumpy old fool like me.' He sat down creakily, and went on to explain.

'It's my chest, d'you see. They want to give me a check-up, give me injections and that, to keep me on my feet over the winter. Normally, I'd be back home after a couple of days – but this time that nurse of mine's gone off on her holidays. Won a trip to Tenerife in a competition. So they're going to keep me in there till she gets back.'

Then, remembering what he'd started out to tell them he added, 'Hospital's a place where sick people go to get well.'

'Oh,' said Tati dubiously.

'I don't suppose you'll have time to come and see me there, will you?' Gramps said, scowling ferociously at them both from under his bushy eyebrows.

So, of course, they went.

They were getting quite confident about exploring the town these days. They followed Gramps's instructions and arrived at a huge concrete building with hundreds of windows all looking exactly the same.

'It doesn't look very nice from the outside, does it?' said Daio nervously.

In front of the hospital were a few strips of muddy, trampled grass with sickly shrubs dotted here and there. Between the shrubs stood row upon row of parked cars. The lingering exhaust fumes made the bwganod sneeze.

'Perhaps it's better inside,' said Tati, not very hopefully.

They floated up the front of the building and began peeping through windows, looking for Gramps.

To their surprise and relief, the inside of the hospital was much, much nicer than the outside. Lots of humans in bed, of course: some lying down and looking much iller than Gramps did, even on his bad days. Other humans seemed quite cheerful and were sitting up in bed and talking or reading magazines or watching television. There were bunches of flowers everywhere, in vases, and fruit and chocolates and bottles of squash on the tables next to the beds. The television sets were high up on the wall, where everybody could see them. All the big rooms had pretty curtains and flowery screens. One of the smaller rooms they peeped into had a carpet and comfortable chairs and a drinks machine, and another one even had a real snooker table. (Tati and Daio had watched snooker on Gramps's television, so they knew all about it).

They found the children's ward with its toys and its brightly-coloured pictures on the walls, and on the next floor they saw a nursery, full of very tiny human babies in cribs. Nurses in stiff white caps hurried up and down the corridors. Once, a child in bed looked startled and a bit frightened, until Tati grinned and waved at her – but apart from that, nobody paid any attention to the two bwganod: they were completely invisible.

Gramps was in a long room on the other side of the building. Getting in posed a bit of a problem, because all the big windows were shut. Eventually the bwganod found an open door on the next level, and oozed through.

Gramps's ward was as bright and pretty and as full of flowers as any of the others – but Tati and Daio could see straight away that the humans in it weren't happy. Everybody was very old, there weren't many visitors, and nobody was laughing or chatting.

Gramps himself wasn't in bed, but he was wearing his pyjamas and dressing-gown (without his flat cap, which made him hard to recognise at first), and he looked twitchy and bored. Some of the other old men seemed just as grumpy; others just looked very sad. And many of them had a strange blank expression in their eyes, as though they'd stopped noticing anything, and didn't care what happened to them any more.

Nurses in green uniforms were handing round cups of tea and trying to chat brightly to the patients. Some of the people they talked to smiled and replied, but the moment the nurse went away, their faces went blank and sad again.

'What's the matter with them all?' Tati asked, horrified.

Gramps shrugged. 'Old age, mostly. Some of them have been here for years. I'm lucky, d'you see. I got a home to go back to, and relations in the same street, and a row now and again to keep the adrenalin going – but they haven't got anybody. Nothing to look forward to, d'you see. Just eating and sleeping and watching the television, day in, day out – and that's no sort of a life when you've been active, is it?'

One or two of the old people showed a faint flicker of interest as the two bwganod hovered beside Gramps's chair.

'Can they see us?'

'Dunno,' Gramps said. 'Some of 'em, maybe.'

Tati looked round the room with its orderly rows of beds. 'Don't they ever have any *fun*?'

Gramps shrugged again. 'There's a day room back there, where you can play cards, and chat, and the trolley comes round with the papers every morning ... plenty to do if you can be bothered to make the effort. But most of 'em have lost interest, like. Fair play, them nurses do their best, I'll give 'em that – but ... No. Something a bit different, that's what they need. Bit of real entertainment, bit of a shock, something to take 'em out of themselves, like.'

Gramps was right. The ward was warm and comfortable and the nurses were kind – but humans, like bwganod, needed more than that.

'I wish *we* could do something,' said Daio.

Tati stared at the old men. Through the open door of the day room she could see old ladies looking just as despairing.

'What, though?'

'I don't know,' Daio confessed. 'Pity Eldan's not here. He could do some real magic to cheer everybody up.'

An idea was taking root in Tati's mind. Suddenly her eyes began to sparkle.

'But we don't need magic – not really!'

'What d'you mean?'

'Why don't *we* entertain them, all by ourselves? We could bring a lot of magical things along, like Mami's flowers, or Esyllt's doves ... and do a magic show all on our own!'

Daio's jaw dropped. 'But they wouldn't be able to see us!'

'That's the whole point!' Tati's idea was firmly rooted now, and growing in all directions and blossoming like mad. 'Dewin could teach us some tricks, if we asked him nicely ... he might even lend us those butterflies of his ... we could borrow all sorts of things from people. And Gramps could pretend to be the magician. And not seeing you and me would make the whole thing look like real magic!'

Daio remembered Tati's sheet, and how frightened the big boys had been at the school. But if Gramps were to wave his hand, and garlands of shining flowers began to waft mysteriously through the air, and ribbons and silken scarves began to dance around the room all by themselves, accompanied by clouds of butterflies ... His face lit up.

'Let's do it, Tat. Let's give a magic show!'

Gramps was nodding encouragingly. 'Jiw, that's a good idea, that is.'

'Right, then,' said Tati. 'How about Thursday? That'll give Daio and me three days to practise.'

All at once Gramps became dubious. 'Let's get this straight. You want me to stand up on my hind legs and make a monkey out of myself in front of all this lot while you two jump about, right?' Gramps was shy.

'Oh, come on, Gramps – you'll be great. We'll tell you exactly what to do.'

'You were the one who said it was a good idea,' Daio reminded him.

'Aye ...well ...' Gramps harrumphed a bit. Then he braced himself. 'All right, then. Long as we do it about half-past eight at night. Don't want the whole hospital up here watching. And I won't say nothing to the nurses, just in case. You two just turn up and we'll do the show on the spur of the moment, like.'

They'd been so busy planning the show that they hadn't noticed the nurse who was heading their way with a worried expression on her face. She bent over Gramps's chair.

'Are you sure you're all right, Mr Evans?'

Gramps gave her a thousand-kilowatt scowl, one of his very fiercest. 'Never better, thank you.' Then, when she'd moved away – still looking puzzled and concerned – he murmured, 'Though if they catch me talking to you two much longer, I'll be stuck in here for good. Off you go, now. Thursday night, half-past eight. All right?'

As they flew home over the wood Daio began to have second thoughts about giving a magic show. Suddenly the whole idea didn't seem nearly as brilliant as it had back there in the hospital ward.

'What if it doesn't work? What if nobody'll lend us anything? What if it's no good, and nobody likes it?'

Like Gramps, Daio was having an attack of stage-fright.

'Oh, c'mon Daio, it doesn't have to be a proper *show*, like on the telly, with singing and dancing and all that ... Most of them won't even see us. Gramps can just wander about, making magical things happen. And if we can make them funny as well, it'll be even better.'

They spent the rest of the night thinking up tricks to entertain the old people. By morning, even Daio was enthusiastic again.

'You're right. It's going to be fun,' he said.

Next day Warren and Eleri and Bethan and Sally-Ann came home from school with exciting news. There was a national competition for the best primary school project on nature and wildlife, and their school had entered for it. To get the project off to a good start, the two top classes were going on a nature ramble with their teachers, so as to find out about the countryside in Autumn. They would all be going by bus to one of the farms high up above the Ceirw Valley, and after looking round the farm they were to split up into groups and walk down through the Ceirw woods, collecting things and making lists of the wildlife they saw, and learning to recognise trees. Miss was bringing ten pairs of binoculars along so that everybody could watch birds.

Even tough boys like Warren in the top class were looking forward to the outing because Sir had promised to bring his very expensive video camera with its close-up and telephoto lenses, and was going to let the biggest and most sensible people use it, and show them how to cut and edit the tape afterwards. They were all to take anoraks and wellies and a packed lunch; and also a box with holes in the lid, to put specimens in. Miss had said that a plastic ice-cream tub would do very nicely.

David was the only one of the Mostyn Close children who was left out, because he was in the next class down.

The ramble was fixed for Thursday.

Meanwhile, Tati and Daio were beginning to discover just how complicated life can be when you're trying to organise something which has to be kept a secret. It meant borrowing things from people and telling them – not lies, exactly, just carefully-snipped-off bits of the truth.

'We just want to practise a kind of magic show, that's all,' Tati explained.

And then of course everybody wanted to know when the real show was going to be put on, and whether they could come, too. It was all very awkward.

'I wish we hadn't promised Gramps now,' Tati said despairingly. 'I had to tell Naino we'd do the show next week for her and Taid.'

'Is she going to bake us the honey cakes, though?' Daio wanted to know. They'd decided that they ought to provide refreshments as well.

'Oh, yes. She's baking a whole batch on Wednesday. I told her,' Tati added guiltily, 'that we were going on a picnic with some friends.'

The Bwganhouse, too, knew that something was going on, and kept nudging them and tickling them to make them tell.

'I'll be glad when Thursday's over,' said Daio gloomily.

In fact, as they soon discovered, their problems had only just begun. As they were on their way to bed in the chill dawn of Thursday morning, Mami announced that she and Dadi were going away for the day, to visit some friends and their new Bwganhouse on the far side of the mountains. Growing a new Bwganhouse is a very important occasion for bwganod – and everybody's friends call in to help, and to wish it luck and long life.

'We'd take you with us,' Mami went on, 'except that it's a very long way, and you'd get dreadfully tired. Anyway, weren't you planning to go on a picnic?'

'Uh … Oh, yes,' said Daio.

'Good. That's settled then. Naino's offered to come over and look after Bwganbabi for the day, and keep an eye on things generally. I want you to help her as much as you can, and especially with Bwganbabi.'

Normally they didn't mind playing with Bwganbabi and running errands for Naino. But today, of all days! Their hearts sank.

When Tati and Daio woke up a few hours later, Mami and Dadi had gone, and Naino was already bustling round the Bwganhouse. She was full of plans for the day.

'First of all, you can help me do some more baking for this picnic of yours. I'll need cowslip flowers and rose nectar and some more of my special honey, so I'll give you a list and you can pop out and fetch them from my Bwganhouse. Then perhaps you could give Bwgantaid a hand with the garden. Then after lunch we'll take Bwganbabi for a little float in the wood. What time did you say you were meeting your friends?'

'Oh, my gosh,' Tati groaned when Naino was safely out of earshot, 'and I was going to make garlands this afternoon, with Mami's flowers.'

'We've got to pick up Dewin's butterflies and Esyllt's doves some time today, too,' said Daio. 'Oh, well – I suppose we'll fit it all in somehow.' But he didn't sound too hopeful.

After lunch, Naino decided to have forty winks. Bwganbabi was already asleep in his cradle of leaves.

'Keep an eye on him for me, will you? When he wakes up we'll take him out for some fresh air.'

The moment Naino's eyes were shut, Tati and Daio dashed round to the garden at the back of the Bwganhouse and began making garlands. It took a lot longer than they'd expected, and Mami's magic flowerbed looked a bit bare when they'd finished.

'I didn't think we'd need so many. What's she going to say when she sees that?'

'She won't mind,' said Tati, crossing her fingers and hoping. They hid the garlands in a friendly pine tree near the quarry, and hurried back home to check on Bwganbabi.

He was still asleep. Naino was snoring gently, and the Bwganhouse itself was snoozing comfortably in the warm October afternoon. Outside, the sun was shining and the leaves were golden in the wood.

'This is ridiculous,' said Tati, after she and Daio had hung around for a while, waiting for somebody to wake up. 'We promised to be at Dewin's this afternoon. If we leave it much longer, he might go out.'

Daio glanced irritably at Bwganbabi, who hadn't moved since they'd looked in on him earlier.

'Might as well nip over there now,' he suggested. 'It won't take more than a few minutes.'

So, feeling rather guilty about it, they went.

Dewin was a dwarf, so old and gnarled and wrinkled that he looked like an ancient tree stump. He lived in a grove of rowan trees on the other side of the Ceirw Valley, and he was a clever magician. His butterflies were all ready for Tati and Daio to take away, in cages of woven grass. The butterflies were huge – as big as thrushes – and had beautiful velvety wings in all the colours of the rainbow.

'We'll be ever so careful with them,' Daio told him earnestly.

Dewin stroked them lovingly. 'I'm sure you will,' he said. 'If they get excited and fly off, just whistle, and they'll come back to you. They're excited already, aren't you, my pretties? – Now, why don't you both sit down and tell me what this magic show is all about, and I'll see if there's any of that strawberry cordial left.'

9

Angry Magic

The children from the primary school were having a wonderful time on their nature ramble in the wood. All except Eleri Hughes.

Eleri was miserable. Right from the start, the day had been nothing but trouble as far as Eleri was concerned. Some days are like that, and there's nothing you can do about it.

Eleri's problems had begun with her specimen box. She'd completely forgotten to tell her mother that she needed a plastic tub, and only remembered as she was on her way to bed on Wednesday night. The only container her mother could find at the last minute like that was an enormous, battered old cake tin, the sort that people would have used fifty years ago to store huge Christmas cakes and wedding cakes in. It had belonged to Eleri's grandmother, and Eleri's mother had kept it in case it came in handy one day. But nobody makes cakes that size any more, and the tin was rusty in places and badly scratched, so Eleri's mother had punched holes in the lid and given it to her to take on the ramble. It was so big it stuck out of the top of her duffel bag.

Even Sir had noticed the tin.

'You won't find many fruit-cake trees in this wood, Eleri,' he'd said – which was a marvellous excuse for everybody to giggle like mad and poke fun at her the moment Sir's back was turned.

In the farmyard she'd dropped her clipboard in the

mud. As she was picking it up again, somebody had bumped into her and knocked her over, and as well as getting mud all over herself she'd torn the sleeve of her new anorak on a strand of barbed wire.

From then on things had got steadily worse. Because she'd fallen in the mud, the rest of her group teased her and pretended she smelt bad, and called her a wimp when she got upset. Every time she spotted something pretty or interesting to collect, somebody else pushed her aside and got there first. Bethan and Sally-Ann weren't talking to her, and she didn't know why.

Everybody else in the group had looked through the binoculars at the buzzards perched in a tree – but by the time it was Eleri's turn to look, the birds had flown away. Everybody else had seen the squirrels jumping through the branches, but Eleri had been looking in the wrong place and had missed them. When Miss found a hedge-hog, and picked it up for everybody to see, Eleri had been shaking a stone out of her welly, and so she'd missed that too.

As far as Eleri was concerned, the nature ramble was a complete washout.

At dinner time the teachers led all the groups to the place where they were to eat their packed lunches. It was an old quarry, all overgrown with ferns and wild rose bushes and thick cushions of soft emerald moss. A stream tumbled in little waterfalls over the rocks, and a slender, graceful silver birch tree hung its delicate branches over the water like a princess leaning over to brush her long golden hair.

Because they'd all been picking up brightly-coloured berries and fungi and other things which might be poisonous if you squished them, all the children had to wash their hands carefully before they were allowed to open their lunch packs. (They'd been told never, ever, to put anything they picked in their mouths or lick their fingers after handling things). The teachers had brought soap and towels and a bowl which they filled under a waterfall. The water was icy cold and everybody squealed.

Some of the boys started messing about in the stream when the teachers weren't looking – and of course it was Eleri who got splashed.

Getting wet was the last straw for Eleri. She turned and fled out of the quarry so that nobody would see her crying. She ran a little way up the rough track nearby, and when she'd gone far enough to be private, she sat down on a big stone to cry herself out in peace.

She'd got to the sniff-and-hiccup stage and was drying her eyes on the sleeve of her anorak when something pale and shining seemed to float through the trees at the top of the high bank opposite. Then it vanished behind a pine tree. It was only a glimpse – but Eleri knew what she'd seen. Flowers: huge white-and-golden flowers like waterlilies.

Thoughtfully, she wandered back to the quarry.

'Flowers?' said Bethan incredulously, through a mouthful of sausage roll. 'Don't be daft, Eleri.'

'She's just making it up,' said Sally-Ann. 'Flowers flying through the air? She's off her head!'

After they'd eaten their lunch and picked up all the rubbish to take home, the two classes started to make a map of the quarry, with all the rocks and ferns and trees in their proper places. Eleri's mind wasn't on what she was doing. She was still wondering about those lovely, magical flowers. She *had* seen them, whatever the others said. She hadn't been dreaming, or making it up, and she wasn't off her head. They'd moved out of sight so quickly – almost as though somebody had been flying along and trailing them behind on a string …

Back in the Bwganhouse, Bwganbabi was waking up.

He lay in his cradle for a while, cooing quietly to himself. Then he sang quite loudly, hoping that somebody would come, but nobody did. After a few minutes he rolled over on his tummy and pulled himself up on the branches at the side of the cradle. He rattled the twigs and gave an imperious little shout. The Bwganhouse half woke up, rocked the cradle and shushed him absentmindedly, and then drifted back into its autumnal dream. Even the Bwganhouse got sleepy towards winter-time.

Naino was sound asleep, and didn't hear Bwganbabi at all.

Bwganbabi was too young to fly. He looked round for Tati and Daio, but there was no sign of them anywhere. Then he crawled out from between the branches, flopped down onto the grassy floor and began to wriggle towards the open door.

The children were packing up ready to go home. Chattering and laughing, they trudged up the old track which Eleri had found earlier. Nobody had used it for a hundred years; it was overgrown with ferns and small bushes, and strewn with fallen rocks, but it still led to the farm where the buses were waiting, and once you were on it, you couldn't get lost.

Eleri was the last to leave the quarry.

'Hurry up, Eleri,' said Warren, looking back. 'You'll get left behind.'

Warren and his friends were just passing the steep high bank where Eleri had seen the flowers. All at once, Eleri made up her mind. She'd show them! She'd show everybody! They'd been mean to her all day. Well, nobody would laugh if she arrived back at the bus with a bunch of those huge, lovely flowers to show the teachers!

She waited, hopping on one foot and pretending to take a stone out of her wellington, until Warren and his gang were out of sight. Then, very quickly and quietly, she began to scramble up the bank.

It was harder to climb than she'd expected. The soil was slippery, and the grass and ferns pulled loose when she tried to use them as handholds. Eleri clenched her teeth and struggled upwards.

At the top, a tangle of wild rose bushes blocked her way like a tall hedge. Ignoring the prickles, she pushed through. Those flowers had to be here somewhere!

And then, quite suddenly, she found herself in a little green glade carpeted with soft, velvety moss. In the middle of the glade stood a clump of small trees. Their shiny, silky grey stems were packed so closely together that it reminded her of a funny little house ...

The whole glade was lit by a strange shimmering purple light: Eleri could see the colour out of the corners of her eyes, but not when she looked straight ahead. The most peculiar thing about the light was that every tiny detail of the clearing – every blade of grass, every moss plant, every leafy twig – was as clear and sharp as if someone had drawn it with a pen. A stone by Eleri's feet had little sparkling flakes in it, and was ridged and patterned like the front of a minuscule cathedral. A tuft of moss looked like a tiny, perfect tree.

Once, when she was a lot younger, Eleri had found a pair of her Nan's glasses and had taken them away to play with. When she'd put them on everything had gone blurred – but Eleri had worn them anyway, until she'd finished her game. (Her Nan had been very cross with her when she'd found out, because nobody should ever try wearing somebody else's spectacles).

But now, kneeling in this magical glade and staring in astonishment at perfectly ordinary stones and leaves and grass, Eleri suddenly felt as though she'd been wearing invisible glasses all her life, and that at last they'd come off. For the first time she was seeing things clearly, as they really were.

Then she saw a movement on the grass in front of the clump of trees – and instantly forgot everything else.

For there, lying on its tummy, was a baby.

Like everything else in the clearing, it too was haloed in that shimmery purple light. It was about the size of a smallish doll, and absolutely perfect except that where its feet should have been there was a kind of blur, and then nothing. It stared up at Eleri out of round green eyes. Its little ears were distinctly pointed.

'A *fairy baby*!' Eleri whispered.

Excitement and awe swelled up inside her until she thought she'd burst. If only Sally-Ann and Bethan were here! They wouldn't laugh at her now! Not now she'd found a real, live fairy baby!

'Will you give me three wishes?' Eleri asked. 'Like in the stories?'

The baby rolled over, sat up with an effort and gazed solemnly at Eleri. Its thumb went pop into its mouth. It was adorable.

'Just wait till I tell them about this!' Eleri thought gleefully.

Then, of course, she realised with a sinking feeling inside that once again nobody was going to believe her. They'd tell her she was making the whole thing up, as usual. And once again they'd laugh, and poke fun at her. Eleri felt like bursting into tears out of sheer annoyance.

Eleri wasn't a particularly sensible person. Nowhere near as sensible as Sally-Ann, for example. She was dreamy, and imaginative, and clever, and all of these are good and useful things. But the trouble with Eleri was that she was also a bit spoilt, and therefore lazy and rather silly. She daydreamed when she should have been listening to important instructions, and she let her imagination run away with her until it sent her into a flat panic over nothing at all, and worst of all she expected other people to sort things out for her. Over and over again she got herself into trouble by doing silly things without stopping to think what the result might be.

She did something silly now. Fumbling with haste, she took the tin box out of her duffel bag. She folded her woolly cap to make a comfortable bed; then she picked up Bwganbabi (who was surprisingly heavy and solid for something that looked so shimmery) and laid him tenderly down inside the tin.

He looked a bit startled, and his face puckered up as though he was about to object quite strongly – but when Eleri slipped one of her furry mittens under his head he changed his mind and beamed at her instead. He was a very good baby.

She was picking up the lid when the first horrible doubt entered her head.

After everybody'd seen the baby, what then? How could she get it back here? If she kept it, how would she look after it?

What if the baby was unhappy, and wouldn't eat? How would she know what to feed it on?

Worse still, what if fairy babies had mothers and fathers like human babies? Wouldn't they be upset if their baby went missing?

Eleri struggled with her conscience. She did so want to take the tin back in triumph and show her find to everybody. But perhaps, after all, she'd better put the baby back on the grass where she'd found it. But then nobody would ever know that she'd seen and picked up and cuddled a real, live fairy.

There was a crashing noise in the briars behind her. Eleri jumped and stifled a scream. But it was only Warren, come to look for her.

'Eleri Hughes, what the heck d'you think you're doing? You're supposed to be on the bus!'

Eleri was too delighted to see him to notice how cross he was.

'Warren, look what I've found! A real, live, fairy baby!'

Warren was a kind boy, in spite of acting tough. When he'd got to the bus and realised that Eleri was missing, he'd disobeyed the teachers' instructions and sneaked back to look for her. He didn't want her to get into any more trouble: he knew she'd had a bad day. Being a good

Cub Scout, he'd followed her trail. And here she was, playing with imaginary fairies!

He glanced into the tin. All he could see were the cap and the furry mitten, slightly crushed.

'Honestly, Eleri, you need shooting! You know we weren't supposed to wander off on our own! Now we'll *both* get a row! I thought you might've sprained your ankle or something. I should have known you'd end up doing something dippy! C'mon, let's get back to the bus before Miss finds out.'

'Warren,' Eleri wailed, tears of indignation welling up in her eyes.

And then the worst happened. Roused by the voices, the Bwganhouse woke up. In a flash, it realised that Bwganbabi wasn't in his cradle, and that there were humans outside. With a roar of anger, it attacked.

All Warren and Eleri knew was that suddenly the peaceful, sunlit glade had gone pitch-dark and was full of noise and writhing branches. Terrified out of her wits, Eleri dropped everything and ran. Warren paused just long enough to scoop up Eleri's duffel bag and jam the lid on the tin – and then he, too, ran as though wolves were after him. Briars coiled round their ankles and whipped their faces as they plunged through the thicket; even the ferns and grasses on the steep earthen bank seemed to clutch at them as they slid down. They pelted up the track and didn't even pause for breath until they'd reached the top.

In the lane, they met one of the teachers. He was very angry – mainly, of course, because he'd been so worried.

'Where on earth have you two been? You know perfectly well you weren't supposed to go off on your own. You could have got lost, or badly injured. Do you realise you've kept us waiting for nearly twenty minutes? I'll have to report you both to the Headmaster.'

The bus was full up. There was no room for Eleri, so she had to sit in the front seat with Miss. Everybody booed when she climbed in.

Warren's friends had kept a seat for him at the back. As he pushed past Eleri he dropped her duffel bag and the biscuit tin onto her lap.

Eleri went cold with horror. The baby was still there!

She tugged frantically at the teacher's sleeve. "Miss! Please, Miss ..."

'Not now, Eleri.' The teacher was talking to the driver, and looking anxiously at her watch.

'But, Miss ...'

'I said, not now, Eleri. You've caused enough trouble as it is.'

The bus lurched forwards, and Eleri had to grab the tin

to stop it sliding off her lap. She cradled it protectively as the bus began to bump down the rutted lane. All at once the dreadfulness of what she'd done struck her like a thunderbolt.

She'd stolen somebody's baby!

'But it wasn't my fault,' she told herself. 'It was Warren. He picked the tin up, not me!'

But all the time she knew perfectly well whose fault it really was. If she hadn't put the baby in the tin in the first place ... if she hadn't *wanted* to steal it ...

And now the angry magic would come looking for her. What on earth was she to do?

10

Kidnapped

Tati and Daio were finding it difficult to get away from Dewin's house without hurting his feelings. Dewin loved having visitors, and now that the summer was over and his rowan trees were falling asleep, he was a bit lonely. Out of politeness the two bwganod had to stay for a cup of strawberry cordial and freshly-baked scones spread with blackberry jelly.

'When am I going to see this show of yours, then?' Dewin wanted to know. 'Haven't been to a Noson Lawen in years.'

'Um … next week, I think,' said Tati. 'We'll let you know in plenty of time. We just wanted to borrow your butterflies to practise with.'

Before they left, Dewin gave Tati a present: a circlet of rowanberries and golden leaves to wear on her head. It was very pretty.

As they flew back over the wood the sunlight was fading. They saw Warren and Eleri hurrying back towards the waiting bus, and the teacher coming down the lane to meet them.

'I've seen those two somewhere before, haven't I?' said Tati.

'Butcher's friends, I think,' said Daio. 'They were in Esyllt's quarry earlier on. Wonder what they were doing in our wood?'

It didn't take them long to find out.

The glade around the Bwganhouse was in an uproar.

Naino was wringing her hands and crying. Taid was stomping about and shouting terrible threats while trying to comfort Naino at the same time. The Bwganhouse itself was incoherent with rage and grief.

'*Where were you*?!!' everybody shrieked when they saw Tati and Daio.

For a few minutes Tati and Daio couldn't make any sense out of what the others were saying, except for the fact that Bwganbabi was missing.

'But he can't have gone far,' Tati said. 'He can't fly yet, and everybody round here knows him!'

It was then that the Bwganhouse finally managed to convey to them what had actually happened.

'*Kidnapped*?' gasped Daio.

He and Tati stared at one another, utterly appalled. If they hadn't sneaked off to Dewin's house ...

Naino was blaming herself just as much. 'If I hadn't gone to sleep ...'

And the Bwganhouse was sunk in a terrible dejection which made it quite clear to everybody that it blamed itself most of all.

'And what your Mami and Dadi are going to say when they get home, I daren't think,' Naino sobbed.

In a flash, Tati remembered the two human children they'd seen scurrying towards the bus: the boy carrying the tin box and the girl limping and holding her side ...

'C'mon,' she said to Daio. Leaving Dewin's precious butterflies with Naino and Taid, they flew to the farm.

But the yard was empty. The buses had gone.

When the bus reached the school, it was nearly a quarter to four. All the parents were waiting outside. They looked worried and cross.

The teachers hustled the children inside and into the Nature Room.

'Right. Thanks to Eleri Hughes, we won't have time to sort anything out this afternoon. Put all your boxes and specimens and notebooks on the table – we'll look at them in the morning. Eleri – where are you going with that tin?'

'Sir, I've got to take it home, it's got a …'

'I'm sure your mother won't mind if it stays here until tomorrow. Just leave it on the table with the others.'

'But Sir, there's a …'

'Come on, Eleri, don't be silly. Whatever's inside will be perfectly all right until the morning. It's all going back to the wood tomorrow, anyway.' And he took the cake tin from Eleri's hands and put in on the top of the pile. Then he shooed everybody out and locked the Nature Room door. Since the break-in, all the inside doors were locked at night, as well as the outside ones.

Eleri was frantic. Tears welled up in her eyes and trickled down her face. She grabbed the teacher's sleeve.

'But Sir, there's a baby in it! A real, live baby!'

The teacher had had quite enough of Eleri for one day. He was trying to listen to a dozen other people at the same time and answer all their questions, and as far as he was concerned, Eleri was just being silly again.

'Oh, for Heaven's sake, Eleri,' he snapped. 'Right, you lot. Everybody out. Your parents have been waiting for half an hour already. I'll answer all your questions in the morning.'

Eleri was beginning to learn that the trouble with being silly and scatterbrained most of the time was that when a real emergency turned up, nobody paid any attention to anything you said.

She was unusually silent in the car on the way home. Bethan and Sally-Ann made up for it by chattering nineteen to the dozen, so Sally-Ann's mother didn't notice.

At home, the television was on and her mother was making her tea.

'What's the matter, love?' her mother asked when Eleri didn't seem to want to eat.

'Just a bit tired, that's all,' Eleri said. Then, in case her mother started asking awkward questions, she added hastily, 'We had a smashing time, though.'

After tea her mother bustled away to give their baby his bath. Eleri sat in front of the television and tried desperately to think of a way of rescuing the fairy baby and taking him back to the wood. She'd had plenty of time by now to imagine how her mother would feel if somebody'd kidnapped *their* baby. The very idea made her feel sick inside.

Perhaps the fairy baby was getting hungry and cold and wet in his tin box. Perhaps he was frightened at being left all alone in the dark. Perhaps he was crying ...

Eleri got up. She had to tell *somebody* what had happened. There was no point in trying to explain things to her mother or her father: they simply wouldn't believe her. They'd think she was coming down with 'flu, or the measles or something, and send her straight to bed. Even Warren hadn't been able to see the baby.

The only person she could think of who might just listen was David from next door.

She tiptoed into the hall and put on her coat and woolly cap. Then she let herself out of the back door, closing it very quietly behind her.

Miraculously, David was outside in the garden shed, feeding his rabbits.

'Hello. What was the nature walk like?'

Eleri burst into tears. Between hiccups and sobs, she told David about the kidnapping.

In spite of being the youngest, David was in some ways the most sensible of all the Mostyn Close children. He knew perfectly well just how dopey and scatty Eleri could be, and how she loved to make up weird stories. But this story, he could tell, was different. Eleri was really frightened, and very upset. All at once he remembered the pale misty shapes they'd seen in the Old Ironworks, and the eerie laughter.

'Honestly, Eleri,' he said severely. 'You need your head read. Picking up a baby like that and running off with it! What a daffy thing to do!'

Eleri's tears dried up like somebody turning a tap off at the mains.

'You *believe* me?'

'Course I do.' David thought for a bit and then said hopefully, 'P'raps it's magicked itself out of that box by now, and gone back home.'

'It was so small, though,' Eleri said. 'What if it couldn't? I mean, we can walk and talk, but babies can't.'

David was already wearing his coat and scarf. The evening had turned frosty again, and the shed was cold.

'Only one way to find out. We'll go back to the school and tell Mr Johnson your mam needs the cake tin. C'mon.' Outside, it was getting dark. The street lights were coming on in a long string down the main road. David and Eleri scuttled off round the corner of Mostyn Close, hoping that nobody would see them, or worse still, stop them to ask them where they were going.

Tati and Daio had called in at the estate once already, to look for Butcher. He wasn't there, so they'd flown to the school. By then, of course, all the children had gone home. Now they were on their way back to Mostyn Close in the hope that Butcher might be available, and able to help.

On the main road they spotted two small figures hurrying towards the town.

'It's them!'

'One of them,' Daio said. 'The other one was bigger.'

'One's enough! C'mon!'

David and Eleri came to an abrupt, terrified halt. Their hearts did back-flips and their knees turned to jelly.

Two misty, purple-haloed figures were hovering right in front of them, blocking their path. The figures had enormous green eyes and pointed ears, and they both looked furiously angry.

'*What have you done with our baby?*' Tati snarled.

Eleri couldn't speak. Her mouth opened and shut, but no sound came out.

'Well?' snapped Daio.

'In the sch-sch-school,' Eleri croaked.

David's heart had started beating again, very fast, with wonder and excitement. He forgot to be afraid. Bwganod *did* exist, after all – and he, David Williams, was talking to them!

'We can see you!' he said joyfully.

Tati was a bit taken aback. 'So?'

'That's the whole *point*!' David explained. 'Nobody else could see the baby, except Eleri. And she didn't mean to steal it, she was just playing with it. And then something horrible came out at them, and Warren picked up the tin and they ran away. Eleri didn't even know Warren *had* the tin until they got into the bus, and then it was too late. Nobody would listen to her, and she's been worried sick. We're going back to the school now, to see if Mr Johnson'll let us have the tin back.'

'I did *think* about stealing it,' Eleri admitted truthfully. 'But then I knew it'd be wrong. I was going to put the baby back on the grass where I found it, only there wasn't time. I was just being silly. I promise I'll never be silly, ever again!'

David looked a bit sceptical at this, but didn't say anything.

Tati glared severely at Eleri. 'We've been worried sick,
too,' she said.

'I know,' said Eleri in a small voice. 'And I'm sorry … I
really am.'

'Okay, let's not waste any more time,' said Daio, taking
charge. 'Back to the school. You'll have to come with us,'
he told the children, 'to talk to this Mr Johnson person.'

They hurried down the road in the gathering dusk, the
two human children running and trotting in turns, and
the two bwganod floating effortlessly alongside.

'Can't you go any faster?' Daio said unkindly.

'N-no,' Eleri panted. 'We're doing our best.'

David was dying to ask the bwganod all sorts of

questions about themselves, but he was soon too breath-less to speak.

But when they got there, the primary school was empty and dark. Mr Johnson and the cleaners had locked up and gone home.

David and Eleri collapsed in a heap on the front steps, feeling sick with disappointment. Tati and Daio flew round the school, looking for an open window, or even a fairly wide crack in a door. But since the break-in every single window had been fitted with special locks and was securely shut. The door panels had been replaced with strengthened glass which had wire netting inside it.

They peered through the window of the Nature Room. They could all see the cake tin on the table because of the lights of the estate. It sat there surrounded by other boxes and plastic bags and branches of rowan.

'Even the little window in the cloakroom's locked,' Tati said miserably.

David was puzzled. 'You mean – you've been here before?'

'Once,' Daio said – and in spite of their worries, the bwganod exchanged a private grin.

And then all four of them froze. Because now they could hear, faintly but distinctly, the sound of Bwganbabi crying. Eleri went cold inside.

'What about the keyholes?' David suggested.

Daio shook his head. 'Metal,' he explained. 'We daren't touch iron. It makes us helpless. We can't disappear, or change shape, or anything.'

In fact the whole school was like an iron cage – and Bwganbabi himself was inside another one (because tins, of course, are made of steel with a coating of tin inside, and steel is made of iron). Even if the bwganod had managed to wriggle in through a crack, they wouldn't have been able to do anything without human help.

91

In sheer desperation David picked up a stone and hurled it with all his strength at the window of the Nature Room. It bounced off, making the whole window shiver.

'Plate glass,' he said. 'We'd need an axe to smash that.'

'Where does this Mr Johnson live?' asked Tati, but David and Eleri didn't know.

'On the estate somewhere,' Eleri said. 'We could go round and ask.'

'Trouble is,' David said unhappily, 'nobody'd believe us.' He made a face. 'There'd be an awful fuss, and they probably wouldn't open up the school anyway.'

Tati and Daio and Eleri knew exactly what he meant. It wasn't difficult to imagine the scene: Mr Johnson coming to the door in his shirt-sleeves and slippers, annoyed at being disturbed like this; curt and suspicious.

'The school? What d'you want to go to the school for, at this time of night? Do your parents know where you are?' And then the phone calls. Fathers arriving in cars, angry and puzzled, asking too many questions and not believing any of the answers ... All four of them shuddered.

'I could try and steal an axe,' David offered, looking across at the backyards and gardens of the estate.

'They've got alarm bells,' Eleri said, surprised at herself for remembering. 'Mum's in the PTA. They had a collection, after the break-in.' Her eyes went wide and horrified. 'They'll put us in jail!'

Tati and Daio flew round the school once more to see if they'd missed any possible way in.

'Any luck?' said Eleri hopefully when they returned.

Daio shook his head.

'My Nan saw bwganod once,' Eleri said. 'She'd have helped us – only she's away in Wolverhampton, with my Aunty Elen.'

And Gramps couldn't have helped, even if he'd been at home instead of in hospital.

'It's no good,' Tati said despairingly. 'We're going to need big magic for this. Let's go and see Dewin again.'

Daio thought that was the best suggestion anybody'd made all evening.

David got up from where he'd been sitting. He was cold and stiff and tired. 'I suppose we'd better go home, then,' he said glumly.

Daio looked at the two shivering human children. They were all right, once you got to know them.

'Might as well,' he said kindly. 'You've done all you could. It's up to Tati and me from now on.'

'Thanks for helping, anyway,' said Tati.

'Will you let us know what happens?' Eleri asked anxiously. The bwganod nodded.

'If you want us for anything,' David said, 'you know where we live.'

And rather forlornly, he and Eleri began the long walk home.

11

The Trouble with Iron

Back at Dewin's house, Tati and Daio poured out the whole story: Gramps, the hospital, Bwganbabi, the children and the locked-up school. Dewin was shocked, but he didn't scold them – the situation was too serious for that. He just shook his head, and looked very grave indeed.

'Iron,' he mused. 'You'll need stronger magic than mine to break *that* spell. Wood and stone I can mould and move – but iron, and plastic, and the works of man – never.'

Tati shivered, thinking of Bwganbabi shut up in that box: hungry, helpless, crying ... And what if all that iron changed him in some way, so that he'd never be able to fly, or change shape, or be a normal bwgan ever again?

What if he got ill, and died?

Tati fought down panic. 'Who else can we ask?'

Dewin thought deeply. 'None of us lesser ones,' he admitted. 'Elves, maybe. Gwrach y Rhibyn might be able to do it – but it'd cost you.'

Daio gulped. 'We'll just have to try, that's all.'

'She might be in a good mood, you never know,' Tati said hopefully.

Gwrach y Rhibyn was not in a good mood. She rarely was. She glowered at Tati and Daio from beneath her draggled green hair, and spat out pondweed.

'So baby brother got kidnapped, did he? And who was supposed to be looking after him while Mami and Dadi were out enjoying themselves, eh? Tell me that.'

Tati and Daio hung their heads.

94

'Well, now,' the witch continued, looking very sly, 'I've always fancied a nice dry Bwganhouse to live in over the winter. So this is what you'll do. You'll tell your Naino and your Taid that I'm willing to do a swop with them. I'll move into their house and they can come down here and live in my swamp.'

Tati and Daio gaped at her, horrified.

'B-but that's not *fair*!' Daio protested.

The witch shrugged. 'Suit yourselves. That's the bargain, take it or leave it. D'you want your baby brother back or not?'

Tati was appalled. The thought of Naino and Taid having to leave their lovely Bwganhouse and move into Gwrach y Rhibyn's disgusting smelly swamp made her want to cry. And it was all her fault – hers and Daio's.

'Can you really magic iron?' she asked desperately.

For some reason this question made Gwrach y Rhibyn look even slyer and shiftier than before. 'A bargain's a bargain,' she said. 'Swop houses first, and then we'll see.'

Daio was on to her like a shot. 'We'll see? That's not good enough! You get Bwganbabi home safe and well – and *then* we'll talk about swopping!'

The witch snarled. 'You watch your mouth, boyo, or something very nasty's likely to happen to you!'

'I don't think you *can* magic iron, can you?' said Tati suddenly. 'It's all a trick, isn't it?'

The witch hissed and spat, and began to submerge beneath the oily black water. 'Curses on the whole lot of you! What d'you want to come round here for, pestering a poor helpless old woman without so much as a dry roof over her head?'

'She can't,' said Tati, resigned. 'We'll have to think of something else.'

They sat on a branch overhanging the farm track, and

thought and thought until their brains were curdling with the effort.

'The Elves would have to be away, of course,' said Tati glumly.

'Typical,' said Daio in disgust. 'They're never around when you actually *need* them.'

'We should have risked that axe,' said Tati. She'd never felt so helpless.

All at once they became aware of noises in the under-growth close by. Somebody was approaching – somebody crashing his way through the dry bracken and whistling an extremely complicated Irish slip jig with all the grace notes. The ferns parted, and a little dancing figure came into view, hopping and stamping his feet to the rhythm of the tune. He was dressed all in green, and perched on top of his curly brown head was a green pointed hat.

Tati and Daio stared in utter disbelief. He was the last person in the world they'd expected to see just then.

At the foot of their tree the little man stopped. A brown bearded face with rosy-apple cheeks tilted upwards, and a pair of very bright blue eyes gazed up at them in twinkling astonishment.

'Well, now! What's up with the pair of yez? Never a word of welcome and faces on yez like a bad shmell.'

'Seamus!' they yelled, and hurled themselves at him, nearly crushing him with hugs.

'That's enough, now. Shtop that. Shtop that,' the leprechaun said, pretending to be cross (but he was pleased really).

He'd come over from Ireland for the weekend.

'There was this fella in a bar in Cork – my word, he was a big lad, a giant, and no mistake. And off to London to seek his fortune that very day, so he was. So I thought to meself, I'll maybe go with him now, and have a drink and a bit of a chat with me friends over the other side. Why not, I thought, I'll hitch a lift and himself none the wiser. Now a pocket is a fine place to hitch a lift, but not when it has a hole in the bottom, which I became aware of when your man got up on his hind legs and I started sliding down inside his trousers. However, my downward progression was brought to a halt by the turn-up of his sock, and I stayed there as snug as a bug all the way over. You could say I came over by *boot*.'

The hardest thing about having a conversation with Seamus was to get him to stop talking and listen. Tati and Daio did their best to get a word in edgeways, but it was impossible.

'Seamus!' Tati shrieked at last, 'shut up!', and burst into tears.

Once he understood the problem, Seamus became serious and thoughtful. 'A tin box, you say? And locks and bolts all over the place?'

'Can you magic iron, Seamus?' Daio begged.

Seamus blew through his whiskers in a baffled sort of way, and regretfully shook his head. 'I can not. Gold and silver I can hold and hoard, but iron, and tin, and the works of man, never.'

There was a moment of dreadful, defeated silence.

'Isn't there *anybody* who can help us get Bwganbabi back?' Daio asked miserably.

Seamus scratched his beard and thought. 'Well now,' he said at last, 'your best bet, as I see it, is to go straight to the Court of the King of the West, where the Great Ones are, and get help from the High Magic there.'

They stared at him with dawning hope.

'Is it far? Will it take us long to get there?'

'Yes and no,' said Seamus. 'Sure it's a long, long way, but it takes no Time at all. No Time in *this* world, you understand.' 'How do we get there?' Daio said eagerly.

Tati was feeling nervous. 'Will you come with us, Seamus?'

The leprechaun shook his head. 'Ye'll have to climb the rainbow, my sweet. Bwganod can do it. Leprechauns, no. There's a wee bit of a weight problem, d'ye see.'

Tati and Daio did see. Unlike them, Seamus was *solid*.

'But where do we find a rainbow at this time of night?'

Seamus thrust his hand into his pocket and pulled out his penny whistle. It looked just like an ordinary flageolet or penny whistle, but in fact it was made of pure gold. 'Easiest thing in the world,' he boasted. 'One more thing, though. Ye'll need a few gifts. It's the polite thing to do, when you're visiting Royalty, to take along a present or two.'

They gaped at him in dismay. 'But nothing we've got is good enough for a King,' said Tati.

'We've got Mami's flowers, made into garlands,' Daio reminded her.

'And Naino's honey cakes, I suppose,' said Tati. '*Nobody* bakes honey cakes like Naino.'

'That'll be just grand,' Seamus beamed. 'Now, remember. Watch your step when ye get there. I've heard it's a chancy kind of a place. You'll need to keep your wits about you.'

They rushed to the Bwganhouse to collect the garlands and the honey cakes, and were back in record time. Seamus put his whistle to his lips.

'Ready?'

They nodded.

'Here we go, then.' And he began to play the tune that calls up the rainbow.

12

Over the Rainbow

Seamus played his whistle better than the Champion of All Ireland. The notes rippled and danced like a pure, clear stream tumbling over waterfalls. The tune he played was the most beautiful tune in the world, but the moment it stopped you couldn't remember one note of it. Magic tunes are like that.

As he played, a pale, shimmering rainbow began to form at his feet. It grew and grew until the arch disappeared into the dark sky above the tree tops.

'Off ye go now,' said Seamus. 'Quick as ye can. I'll hold the rainbow for yez with the music until ye get to the top. They'll see yez back home safely from the Court of the King. Good luck to yez!'

The rainbow was a stairway, as fragile and as transparent as a soap bubble. But the steps, of course, were no help to the bwganod, because of not having feet. Seamus had thought of that, however. Somehow he'd managed to arrange a handrail on one side.

Carrying the garlands and the basket of cakes, the two bwganod began to climb by floating, and pulling themselves up using the handrail. When they were well above the tops of the trees, they paused and looked down to wave. Already Seamus looked very small and far away. Then they turned their faces upwards, to where the long steep slope of the rainbow vanished into the dark.

Climbing the rainbow wasn't nearly as easy as it sounds, even for bwganod. As they got further and further away from the ground, floating got harder until they were having to drag themselves up, hand over hand. Slowly the darkness around them began to dissolve, as though dawn was breaking. As the light grew the rainbow began to shine in all its brilliant, dazzling colours, and made their eyes hurt.

Tati looked down. The world lay far beneath them, curved like the top of a tennis ball. She could see mountain ranges and shaggy green forests and coastlines and the glittering sea.

'For heaven's sake don't let go,' she warned Daio. 'If we slip off up here we'll float forever and never get down!'

Up they climbed, up and up. Their arms and shoulders began to ache, and their hands were soon sore with gripping the slippery rail. Tati had slung the handle of the basket over her arm, and it pinched and bruised her as it swung.

'Keep going,' Daio panted. 'Seamus is holding the rainbow, remember.'

They struggled upwards.

'Hope this King person's worth it,' Tati muttered.

'He'd better be,' said Daio grimly.

Suddenly the rainbow disappeared into a thick white cloud just above their heads. A few metres higher, and the cloud was all around them – a dense, chilly mist through which the rainbow glowed bravely. And then, without any warning, the mist vanished away, and the two bwganod found themselves in brilliant sunshine, with a deep blue sky overhead. They'd reached the top of the rainbow.

They were floating above an immense sea of clouds stretching as far as their eyes could see in all directions except straight ahead. There, the rainbow curved up out of the clouds like a bridge and down again onto dry land a few metres away.

Tati and Daio paused, and stared in astonishment.

In front of them was exactly what you'd have expected to see if the clouds had been a real ocean – a wide sandy beach. At the top of the beach was a line of dunes, and behind that, a thick, dark forest.

The beach was deserted. Nothing moved anywhere, or made a sound: no seagulls in the sky, no waves breaking, nothing scuttling over the sand. There was no sign of anything alive anywhere – except for that line of distant, dark trees. The silence was eerie.

'Where's the King, then?' said Tati in dismay.

Daio was scanning the shoreline. A little way over to their right he could see a faint track in the sand. It led up the beach and seemed to be aiming for the forest's edge.

'Perhaps we're meant to go up there.'

They floated up the gently sloping beach and through the dunes to where the forest began. The trees were enormous, and so ancient that their gnarled and sagging trunks were twisted round each other, each one leaning heavily on its neighbours. The bwganod had never seen their kind before. Their branches too were twined and twisted in a dense, thorny tangle like a colossal hedge. When they felt Tati's touch, the gaps closed up even tighter. Old and sullen magic rippled along the barrier, like an electric fence.

'They won't let us through!' said Tati in a panic. 'They don't know us! They won't talk to us … What do we do now?'

'There's an opening a bit further along,' Daio called.

The opening was a narrow gap in the forest wall, round which the branches tangled to form a rough arch, like a doorway into darkness.

'This whole place gives me the creeps,' said Daio with a shiver. 'This can't be the way to the King's Court. Seamus must have made a mistake.'

'This is the path, all right,' said Tati. 'Look!' Above the arch, the branches were woven into the shape of a crown.

102

She stretched her hand warily into the gap, but no magic shorted across to prevent her. Heartened, she launched herself into the gloom – and got a nasty surprise. She couldn't fly. The power of the ancient trees was like a crushing weight which hurled her to the ground.

'I can float okay,' Daio said. 'It's flying forwards they don't like.'

'We'll just have to haul ourselves along, then,' Tati said grimly, and grabbed hold of a branch. It didn't seem to object. 'Like climbing the rainbow all over again.'

There was no light inside the forest. The path was a tunnel, walled in and roofed over by the crowding, menacing trees. At first they could see the tunnel entrance behind them – a bright hole which got smaller and smaller as they moved deeper into the gloom. Then the path turned a corner and the hole disappeared. Suddenly the bwganod were in pitch darkness and couldn't see a thing. Even a bwgan's eyes were useless in that blackness.

Scared and bewildered, they came to a halt.

'I don't like this much, Tat,' Daio said in a shaky voice. 'Let's go back.' But he'd lost his sense of direction already; he didn't know for certain which way he was facing, or even where Tati was.

Tati was scared, too, but the sound of Daio's voice – thin and quavering with fright – triggered something deep inside her which until then she hadn't known she possessed. It wasn't courage, exactly – but it was the next best thing: a kind of angry stubbornness that absolutely refused to be beaten. Gramps would have recognised it instantly.

If this was a trick of the forest, Tati thought, to stop them reaching the King of the West – then it wasn't going to work. No way.

'Hang on to me,' she told Daio firmly. 'Don't let go. This is the right path, and they're not going to put us off.'

Daio groped around in the dark and found Tati's sleeve.

'Right,' said Tati briskly. 'Let's go.'

As she pulled herself defiantly forwards, something very surprising happened. A faint ruby glow began to shine out of her hair. The glow brightened until they could see the trees on either side of them, and the path ahead.

'What on earth …?' said Tati, but Daio's heart leapt.

'It's the rowanberries! It's Dewin's crown!'

Tati had almost forgotten it was there. She put her hand to her hair in astonishment – and then she noticed that Daio, too, had begun to shine. His light was pale and silvery.

'Mami's flowers!' she gasped. 'You're carrying the garlands!' And they both began to laugh.

With their laughter, the light sprang up brightly all round them, ruby and silver, banishing the menacing gloom. The trees had never seen light or heard laughter before, and they shrank back a little from the path.

'They're shining for us!' Daio said. 'But you had to be brave first! Oh, well done, Tat!'

'Well, don't just hover! C'mon!'

They'd gone about a mile along the path and were beginning to feel extremely pleased with themselves, and even a bit smug – when all at once, out of the darkness ahead, there came a savage, deafening, bellowing roar which froze their blood. Their frail lights trembled and went out.

Something huge and black and shaggy was blocking the path. They could just see it because it too was shining, very faintly, with a dull bluish light. Massive hairy arms hung down almost to the ground; little red piggy eyes peered greedily at the two bwganod, and a vast mouth opened like a cavern, exposing rows of very long, very sharp teeth.

It was a Troll.

'You no go,' the Troll snarled in a voice like a rumble of thunder. 'Me Guardian. You no go.'

Trembling with fright, Tati and Daio backed away.

'Me Guardian,' the Troll said again. 'Me eat you.'

'Oh, my gosh,' muttered Daio, 'now what?'

Tati was thinking fast, trying to remember all she'd ever heard about Trolls, which wasn't a great deal. One thing she did recall was that they weren't very bright. And there was something else, too …

She curtseyed very low. 'Oh, Great Lord Troll, Lord of the Forest,' she said. 'Please let us pass. We're much too little and thin for you to eat.'

Daio caught on fast. He bowed, elf-fashion. 'Let us pass, Lord Troll. We bear urgent messages for His Majesty the King of the West.'

'Uh?' said the Troll, and bent down to peer closely at the bwganod. You could tell he was puzzled by all this bowing and curtseying. It wasn't what he was used to at all.

'Me Guardian,' he said. And then, like a stuck gramophone record, 'You no go. Me eat you.'

'Nice try, Tat,' Daio muttered under his breath. 'Pity it didn't work.'

'Give me a chance, will you?' Tati hissed indignantly. She tried a different approach. 'We've brought a gift for the Lord of the Forest,' she said. 'A special present, just for you.'

Daio was alarmed. 'Hang on a minute,' he whispered. 'What d'you think you're doing?'

'Shut up. Let me handle this.' She'd already made up her mind. Taking a deep breath for courage, she lifted Dewin's little crown of rowanberries off her head, and held it out in front of her. The berries blazed with their ruby light, and the leaves glistened like living gold. It was the prettiest, most magical thing Tati had ever possessed, and her heart ached at the thought of giving it away. But Bwganbabi was much, much more important.

The Troll's eyes widened. Not many people know this, but Trolls love shiny, glittery things. 'Pretty,' he said.

'It's for you,' Tati insisted. 'Yours to keep.'

The Troll stood absolutely still for nearly a minute. What Tati had suggested was a new idea to him, and new ideas take a long, long time to register in the lump of solid concrete which is the brain of a Troll.

'Uh?' he said at last.

Tati's patience gave out. 'Look, here it is. If you want it, you can have it, okay?', and she dropped the little circlet into the Troll's enormous hairy palm.

The Troll stared at the gleaming coronet for a long time before slipping it onto his little finger. He turned his hand this way and that, admiring the shining berries. The vast mouth opened, and the massive shoulders began to shake – the Troll was chuckling with pleasure. Through all the uncounted centuries that he'd been Guardian of this dark and silent path, nobody had ever given him a present before.

'Pretty,' he murmured. 'Pretty, pretty …'

'Now!' Tati whispered. Holding their breath and keeping their fingers crossed for luck, she and Daio sneaked quietly past him into the darkness beyond. The Troll didn't notice. All his attention was focussed on the little shining circlet of berries and leaves.

'Let's hope the light doesn't decide to go out just yet,' Daio muttered as they made their escape.

'Poor old thing,' Tati said indignantly. 'I bet whoever put him here forgot all about him hundreds of years ago. I hope it does go on shining, just to cheer him up a bit.'

'It can't be much of a life,' Daio agreed. 'Pitch black dark the whole time, and nobody to talk to except the odd victim.'

The bwganod dragged themselves along the path, deeper and deeper into the forest. Now Mami's garlands were their only source of light.

On and on they went, until they both began to wonder if they'd ever find a way out again. Perhaps this whole forest was a trap. Perhaps the King of the West didn't exist after all. And yet Seamus had sent them here. Seamus was clever and wise, and they trusted him.

'There's got to be a way out. This path has got to end *somewhere*,' Tati told herself fiercely. Every time she began to lose hope or feel so tired that there didn't seem to be any point in going on, she remembered the frightened, miserable noise of Bwganbabi crying, and all her courage surged back in a furious rush.

She shifted the basket of honey cakes from one arm to the other and back again. It seemed to be getting heavier every minute.

'Let's do a swop for a bit,' Daio suggested.

As Tati lifted the garlands over her head (they were actually heavier than the basket, but easier to carry), she noticed that their pure white glow seemed to have faded a bit, and turned slightly greenish. She looked at Daio suspiciously.

'Are you okay? Not feeling sick, or anything?'

'I'm fine,' Daio assured her – and then he noticed the difference too.

'Well, I'm all right, so it can't be me.' Tati looked round her in perplexity – and made a discovery.

'The whole wood's getting lighter – look!'

She was right. The shadows were thinner, you could see further into the gloom on either side of the path, and in the distance the trees were faintly tinged with pale green.

'We've made it!' Daio was exultant. 'We're nearly there! C'mon!'

Tati stayed where she was. Every instinct she possessed was warning her to be careful.

'Daio – no. Come back!'

'Why, what's the matter?'

'I think,' Tati said slowly, 'it's the wrong sort of light.'

13

Guardians

They moved forwards cautiously. The greenish glow grew brighter. It wasn't daylight: Tati had been right about that. It was a horrible sickly green which made everything look somehow rotten and diseased.

The bwganod rounded a bend in the path – and halted in dismay.

They were looking down a long slope into a vast, dark hollow exactly like a big cave, except that the walls and roof were made of branches instead of rock. A line of the biggest trees Tati and Daio had ever seen marched like pillars down the middle. All the branches tangled together overhead to form a woven roof too dense for sunlight to penetrate. The cavern should have been pitch dark – but it wasn't.

In the far right-hand corner a huge and hideous monster lay sprawled on the ground. Its whole body glowed with intense green light. It was a colossal snake, as thick as the tree trunks that lined the hollow, and so long that even coiled up as it was, it filled nearly a quarter of that immense cave. It had nine separate heads on nine long snaky necks.

Tati and Daio shrank back among the shadows of the path, and exchanged horrified glances. A big stupid Troll was one thing – but nine spiteful serpent heads were not going to be tricked so easily.

The heads were quarrelling amongst themselves. You could hear the hissing commotion quite clearly from where the bwganod were hiding.

'You're a sneak, you are. A nasty, vicious little sneak.'

'Oh, yeah? Hark who's talking, fatso!'

'Why don't you two shut up for ten seconds? Some of us are trying to sleep.'

'Aw, shut up yourself. Who asked you to butt in?'

'Garbage-brain!'

'Gutbucket!'

'Shut up! You're driving us nuts!'

'Don't you tell me to shut up, fishface, or I'll have your guts for garters!'

'Fishface, is it? You're a pig – a big fat greedy pig!'

Tati and Daio shrank back even further into the darkness.

'Talk about a split personality!' Daio murmured.

The quarrelling went on and on. Tati switched her attention from the monster to the cave itself, and the path that led through it. The path zigzagged between the trees in the middle of the cave, and ended at a small arched opening in the gloom of the far left-hand wall.

'How on earth are we going to sneak past that thing?'

'We could just about make it,' Daio whispered excitedly. 'See? With that line of trees down the middle, it's like two caves, not one.'

Tati looked again – and saw that he was right. The monster's body lit up one half of the cavern so brightly that the trees down the centre cast deep shadows across the other half.

'If we keep to the left-hand wall all the way, and climb up quite high, to where the shadows are darkest ...' Daio said.

It was a dangerous plan, and they both knew it. The first bit would be the worst, because they would be in full view of the big snake.

Unless something happened to distract its attention at the crucial moment …

The heads were really fighting now. A hideous squealing and shrieking and snarling filled the air: all nine necks were tangled up in knots, and all nine heads were snapping at each other with long fangs.

'Now!' said Daio. 'Tell the flowers not to shine!'

To Tati's amazement, the light of Mami's flowers obediently went out.

Cautiously, the two bwganod edged out of the tunnel and along the wall of the cavern. The trees didn't stop them climbing up. They'd reached the shadows, and the fighting still hadn't stopped. Pulling themselves along, moving stealthily, almost afraid to breathe, Tati and Daio made their way from shadow to shadow, as high up as they could manage.

They were half-way there. Now they were passing the place where the monster lay coiled on the other side of the central line of trees. Inch by inch they pulled themselves onwards. Now the tree-wall of the cave was curving around to where the exit was. Only a few metres more … and then …

Suddenly the fighting ceased, and there was dead silence in the cave.

Nine heads rose out of the gleaming coils, swaying, questing, searching the gloom with cold eyes. Nine long forked tongues flickered in and out, tasting the air.

'Honey!' the heads hissed greedily. 'Honey! Honey!' and the great sluggish coils began to unwind. The monster had smelt Naino's cakes.

One of the heads spotted the two bwganod and gave a screech of triumph.

'*Dinner!*'

With unexpected and horrifying speed, the huge body reared up and began to slide towards them.

There were only nine heads, but Daio wasn't taking any chances. He swung his arm back and hurled the whole basket as far and as high as he could. Honey cakes showered down all over the floor of the cave, with the basket thumping after.

'*Honey*!' the heads shrieked, and dived in a mad scramble for the cakes.

'*Now*, Tati!' Daio yelled.

The bwganod shot forwards, using every last ounce of their strength. As they plunged through the archway into the dark tunnel beyond, a howl of fury rose from the cavern behind them.

'Faster, Daio, faster!' Tati shouted. Mami's flowers blazed defiantly as they fled.

The giant snake didn't come after them. Perhaps after all the arch was too narrow for it; or perhaps it had orders not to leave the cavern. Whatever the reason, in a few minutes the clamour of the Guardian had died away, and Tati and Daio were once again alone on the dark, silent path in its tunnel of trees.

The bwganod were very tired now. They had no idea how far they'd travelled just by pulling themselves along from branch to branch, but it must have been several miles, at least. Their shoulders were sore, and their arms felt as though they were going to drop off at any minute. They were hungry, too – and worst of all, thirsty. But there were no streams in this forest, and nothing to eat.

Daio gave a groan and dropped to the ground. 'Sorry, Tat. If I don't have a rest, I'll die!'

'But what about Bwganbabi?'

'I know, I know. But didn't Seamus say that being here doesn't take up any time in our world? So we might as well rest – we're not losing anything, are we?'

Tati saw the sense of that. If something else happened, they'd need all the strength and energy they could muster. No good facing danger if you were half-dead with exhaustion.

'Okay, then. Not for long, though.'

They propped themselves up side by side against the bole of a tree. Tati discovered that she didn't have the energy even to take the garlands off. They both flopped, too tired to talk.

Tati thought, So here we are, in a place outside Time, like the Elves. There must be lots of places like this. Places where Time goes faster, and places where Time goes slower. And who's to decide which of these times is the right Time? No wonder the Elves get confused.

Beside her, Daio was sliding down bit by bit until he was curled up on the ground. He was fast asleep.

Her eyes half-closed, Tati thought about the Court of the King of the West. Courts were splendid places, weren't they? – where people wore their best clothes all the time, and everybody was rich and powerful. It suddenly struck her how dirty and scruffy she and Daio must look after all their adventures – and they'd started out in their ordinary, home-made everyday clothes anyway. What would the King think of them when they turned up in this state? Would he even bother to talk to them?

The flowers around her neck glowed brightly, comforting her. She hugged them, knowing that magic flowers wouldn't get crushed or messy or lose their petals, whatever you did. The garlands were the only present they had left now to give to the King. And what were a few magic flowers to a Great One who probably had whole gardens of even more magical flowers to pick whenever he liked?

Without meaning to, Tati fell asleep. At first she dreamt that she was back home in the Bwganhouse and playing with Bwganbabi, who had never been lost after all. Then

113

the dream changed, and she saw Daio fast asleep on the ground, while close by she seemed to hear a slithery, shuffling, snuffling noise. A voice from somewhere far away wailed 'Ai … ai … want shining! *Bad* shining!' Then, quite suddenly, she woke up.

She was all alone. Daio had disappeared.

Tati was bolt upright in an instant. 'Daio! Daio, where are you?'

Surely he wouldn't have gone off on his own without waking her? The garlands were still around her neck – he wouldn't have gone anywhere without light. Something must have happened to him while she was asleep. But what?

The only clues she could find were a tiny scrap of pond-slime, and some wet slithery marks on the path.

She reached up and began pulling herself frantically in the direction the marks led. What a fool she'd been to fall asleep! If Daio was in trouble …

The flower-light warned her just in time. In front of her, and stretching right across the path, was a wide patch of gurgling, smelly swamp.

'Daio!' she called – but there was no answer.

Instead, the swamp began to chuckle and heave itself up – and there, in the middle, sat an old crone as ugly and sly as Gwrach y Rhibyn herself. In fact, the two witches could easily have been sisters – green hair, pondweed slime and all.

Tati was too angry to be scared.

'What have you done with my brother?' she demanded.

The witch giggled, and stroked her long yellow teeth.

'Pretty boy safe with me, in my palace of slime. Your turn now, pretty shining one.'

'No way!' Tati snapped. 'I want him *back*, d'you understand? Now, this minute!'

'Oho,' the witch gloated, rubbing her bony hands. 'Got no choice, you. Come to Aunty, little shining one. Last of the Guardians, I. No one passes *me*!'

She moved one hand over the surface of the water, and for a moment Tati caught a glimpse of pale drowned shapes lying very still in the black depths. The witch grinned slyly from under her dripping hair. 'Come, now ... come ...'

A powerful force began to pull Tati towards the water. She grabbed a branch and resisted it with all her might. Mami's flowers burst into dazzling light – and to Tati's astonishment the pulling-force slacked off so abruptly that she bumped into the tree. The witch hissed and moaned as though the light had hurt her.

'Ai ... ai ...' she sobbed, and thumped her bony fist on her knee, like a spoilt child having a tantrum. 'Want *shining*! *Bad* shining – not fair! Want *nice* shining, not hurt me!'

Now Tati's dream was starting to make sense. She hadn't been asleep – she'd been half-awake, in that strange state between deep sleep and full awareness. The witch had kidnapped Daio, but she hadn't touched Tati because ...

'Mami's flowers wouldn't let you!' Tati concluded triumphantly. And she remembered something Mami had told her long ago. 'They can't be stolen,' Mami had said. 'Only given. Given, with love. Without love, they fade and the light goes out.'

The witch went on snivelling. 'Gold, silver, jewels I have. Nasty cold hard things, no shine for me in my lovely swamp. Want shining flowers.' She rocked herself and wailed. 'Poor old woman, I. Poor lonely old Gwrach in the dark with no shining ...'

'Okay, okay,' said Tati, exasperated. 'I get the message. You want the flowers, right? Simple. Just let me cross to the other side, and let Daio go, and you can have them.'

115

The old Gwrach gave a sudden, evil chuckle – and unleashed a blast of power that should have snatched Tati into the swamp. But Tati hadn't grown up knowing Gwrach y Rhibyn without learning to take precautions. She'd kept her grip on the branch, and Mami's flowers blazed out again to protect her. Tati stayed where she was.

The witch was furiously angry now. 'No give!' she screamed. 'I *take*! Last of the Guardians, I. Take you and boy *and* shining!' She crouched in the swamp, muttering another spell.

'It won't work,' Tati yelled. 'If you take them from us by force, they won't shine for you. They'll die, like everything else you've stolen and hidden down in that swamp of yours! Stealing brings bad luck, didn't you know that?'

The witch paused. Like the Troll, she wasn't very bright. Hate and misery and stealing were the only things she understood. She made a big effort to come to grips with what Tati was telling her.

'*Give* me, then!' she demanded at last, stretching a thin, clawed hand across the water.

'Only if you let Daio and me go,' said Tati firmly.

'No heart, you,' the witch complained. 'Hard as nails, you. Don't care about a lonely old woman in the dark with no shining.'

'Too right,' Tati retorted. 'You give me my brother back, *exactly* as he was before he met you, wide awake and normal in every way …' (She was taking no chances. She knew that with somebody as sly and slippery as a swamp-witch anything could happen if you didn't say exactly what you meant) '… and see us both safely onto the bank on the other side – and no tricks of any kind on either of us – and I'll give you the flowers. Otherwise, no deal.'

The witch sobbed and snivelled. She wanted those flowers very badly. But she also wanted two more victims to add to her tally in the swamp.

116

'Make up your mind,' said Tati, and started to move away, back down the path. The witch gave a howl of distress.

'Wait, wait! I give!'

Tati stopped and waited. The swamp heaved and plopped; something pale shot out of it, like a pip out of a squeezed orange – and there was Daio on the far bank, looking startled and shaking pondweed out of his hair. He was wet and muddy, but otherwise unharmed.

The witch pointed a long finger at Tati. 'Now you.'

Tati swallowed hard. The swamp didn't look any safer than it had a few minutes ago. And could you ever really trust a swamp-witch? Very cautiously, she reached up and grabbed an overhanging branch. There was no force to drag her down. She swung herself across, hand over hand, and joined Daio on the opposite bank.

'Thank you,' she said, and meant it. 'Here, take these flowers as a gift from the bwganod. May they shine forever in your palace of slime.'

She flung the garlands onto the surface of the swamp. They floated there for a moment – delicate, luminous and fragrant – and then, very slowly, they sank, leaving a trail of silver light in the black depths.

Tati was trembling with relief. She looked Daio up and down. 'Are you okay?'

'Fine,' said Daio, grinning. 'I thought I'd had it for a bit there, though. Thanks, Tat.' He did a little spin in the air to show how good he felt. Then he gasped. 'Tati! Did you see that? We're back to normal!'

It was true. Now that they'd passed the last Guardian, the crushing weight of magic which had kept them grounded for so long had lifted clean away. They could fly!

It was wonderful to be airborne again, and free. In the distance was the little bright hole in the darkness that showed the path was indeed coming to an end. Tati and Daio sped towards it, yelling joyously. They burst out of the wood into warm, bright sunlight which dazzled their eyes. For a few minutes all they could do was tumble crazily about in the air, diving and twisting and turning somersaults for the sheer relief of having got through the wood and defeated the Guardians.

Now all they had to do was find the Court of the King of the West, and ask to borrow some High Magic to get Bwganbabi out of his tin box.

14

The King of the West

At last they remembered what they'd come for.

'C'mon,' said Tati, 'Let's go and find this King person.'

The path led out onto a smooth green hillside sloping down into a wide valley. On the left the valley opened out, and turned into a magnificent rocky coast with little white sandy beaches and the real, glittering, blue-green sea. Flocks of sea-birds circled overhead, and the valley echoed with their cries. You could smell the sea from the hill and hear the crash and swish of waves breaking.

Just below the bwganod, on a flat green lawn, there stood a city of tents. Huge silken tents of crimson and azure and gleaming gold, of purple and green and russet and every colour in between. Hundreds of brilliantly-coloured banners fluttered in the sea breeze. They had reached the Court of the King.

Tati looked critically at Daio. 'You look terrible,' she said. He'd managed to rub off most of the mud, and the sun had dried him – but he was still the filthiest bwgan ever to have visited the King of the West.

'You don't look so great yourself,' Daio pointed out indignantly. 'Your hair's all tangled up with twigs and moss, and there's green stuff all down your front.'

Tati's heart sank. It didn't seem fair. They'd come all this way, and braved all those dangers – wouldn't it be awful if nobody let them in to see the King after all, because they were too dirty?

'And we haven't even got any presents for him any more,' she said dolefully.

Daio snorted. 'It's his own stupid fault,' he declared. 'All those Guardians of his – what else does he expect?'

Tati blinked: Daio was absolutely right. And for the first time she began to wonder what sort of a King this was, if getting to see him was so very difficult? How many people, she wondered, had died in that dreadful forest, on their way to ask a favour of the King of the West? And did he care?

Probably not. Or he wouldn't have put the Guardians there in the first place.

And if he didn't care about people dying, then what chance had she and Daio of persuading him to rescue one small Bwganbabi from a tin box?

Tati was very thoughtful as she followed Daio down the long grassy slope towards the city of tents.

As they approached the city, they could see hundreds of richly-dressed people strolling to and fro in the wide green spaces between the tents. There were Elves, stately and golden-haired; magicians in robes of purple; Dwarves, Centaurs, Pookas, Great Ones of every possible kind, all haughty and beautiful and magnificent to behold. But no bwganod. And no children.

Tati and Daio felt small and scruffy and ashamed. They wished they hadn't come.

And now people were beginning to stare at them, and nudge each other, and snigger. Nobody asked the bwganod what they wanted: the courtiers of the King of the West were far too important to speak to a couple of ragamuffin children. Tati and Daio saw the grins and the nudges, and felt awful.

Then the thing they'd been dreading most happened. A soldier in armour, with a long sword dangling at his side, shouted 'Oi! You there!' and began to stride towards them.

'What d'you think you're doing here?' the soldier demanded. 'This is the King's Court, not a backstreet slum. Go on, hop it.'

'We want to speak to the King,' Daio said indignantly.

'We only want to ask him a favour,' Tati pleaded. 'Take us to him, please!'

'A favour? You? Don't make me laugh. We don't want your sort here. Now scram, before you find yourselves in real trouble!'

'But our baby brother's been kidnapped,' Tati said desperately. 'We came all the way here, and passed all the Guardians, to ask the King to help us ...'

But the soldier wasn't listening. He'd grabbed them both by the shoulders and was hustling them away from the tents.

'You've *got* to let us talk to him! Oh, please ...'

Suddenly a new voice broke in on the argument: the kind of voice that expects to be obeyed, with salutes.

'What seems to be the trouble, sergeant?'

The two bwganod twisted round to look. A very tall, broad-shouldered young man was standing behind them. He wore a cloak of russet brown embroidered all over with golden leaves, and a circlet of red gold on his head. His mane of shaggy hair was the colour of winter bracken, and his face was proud and fierce, with keen amber eyes. But when he looked down at Tati and Daio his expression was unexpectedly kind. One of his eyes closed for an instant in a reassuring wink.

The guard let go of the bwganod, and stood to attention.

'No trouble, my Lord. I was just getting rid of these two urchins ...'

'Really?' the Great One said, and although his voice was quiet, it had a dangerous edge to it. 'Didn't I hear them say they wanted to speak to the King?'

The soldier gulped. 'Well, yes, my Lord, but ...'

'It seems a reasonable request to me. I'll take care of it from now on, sergeant. You may go.'

It had begun to dawn on the sergeant that this Great One was not too pleased with the way he'd treated Tati and Daio. He went a bit red, and started to stammer. 'I-I was only ...'

'In future,' said the Great One serenely, 'I hope you'll remember that petitioners of the King are to be treated with courtesy, whoever they are.'

'Y-yes, Lord,' the sergeant said, and sidled away.

'What's a petitioner?' Daio whispered to Tati.

Their new friend had sharp ears. 'Somebody who wants to ask the King a favour,' he explained.

Daio nodded. 'That's us, all right.'

'Will you really take us to see the King?' Tati asked breathlessly.

The Great One smiled. It was a nice smile, and their spirits rose. He held out both hands to them.

'I'll do my best,' he promised. 'As we go, though, why don't you tell me what the problem is?'

They wondered who and what he was. Not an Elf, certainly – though he was as fierce and as lordly as any of that race.

'Are *you* the King of the West?' Tati asked suspiciously.

The stranger laughed. 'No, of course not. You can call me Cern.'

They moved briskly through the crowds of people, and as they went Tati and Daio told Cern the whole story of their adventures from beginning to end. Cern listened and nodded and asked sensible questions, and didn't seem at all shocked, or even amused. It was a bit like talking to a nice, youngish uncle.

Finally he led them into an open space where an immensely tall figure was talking to a small group of extremely important-looking people. Cern let go of the bwganod's hands and strode forwards.

'Sire,' he said, bowing low.

The King turned round. He had long silver hair – the colour of moonlight on storm-clouds – and a silver beard that reached to his waist. On his head he wore a tall jewelled crown, and his robes were the colour of sunset.

'Ah, Cern,' he said, in a voice like a great wind from the sea. 'They told us you were bringing two ragamuffin children to speak with us. Is this, perhaps, some kind of joke?'

'Indeed, no, Sire,' said Cern. 'They are young bwganod. They have risked their lives in the Perilous Wood to reach this place. They are valiant beyond imagining. And they wish to beg a favour of your Majesty.'

The King's eyebrows rose in amused surprise. 'A favour? Of me?'

He stared down at Tati and Daio from his great height, taking in every detail of their appearance: every smear, every mud-stain and every wisp of moss. His lip curled in contempt.

'So. And what is this *favour* you would beg of the King of the Winds and the Ocean? A great gale, perhaps, to crush your little thickets into matchwood? Or shall I command the great sea to rise and flood your miserable little hovels and sweep away all traces of your people for ever? Speak! Don't leave me in suspense!' He was smiling as he spoke, but it wasn't a kind smile, it was almost a sneer. The courtiers began to smile too, in the same sarcastic way, and to snigger behind their hands. Tati and Daio were struck dumb with fear and embarrassment.

'And what gifts have you brought us, as an earnest of good will?'

Somehow, Tati managed to speak. 'N-nothing, your Majesty,' she whispered, and hung her head in shame.

'*Nothing*?' The King's voice was terrifying. Tati and Daio shook like jelly.

'Please, your Majesty,' said Daio, astounded at his own temerity, 'our baby brother's in an iron box, he was kidnapped and ...'

'Kidnapped? My dear child, that's hardly our affair. You have the impertinence to suppose that the King of the West should concern himself with a missing *baby*?'

He threw back his head and began to laugh. All the other Great Ones began to laugh too, until the only people in the group who weren't laughing were Tati and Daio and Cern.

Cern stepped forwards again. 'Sire,' he said seriously, 'I beg you, listen to their story. These two younglings have braved the dangers of the Guardians and have won through all alone, trusting that your Majesty would help them. Surely you can spare a few moments to grant their request?' The

King's laughter stopped as abruptly as it had begun. He glared at Cern.

'This prank of yours is no longer amusing, Lord Cern. You presume too far. Take yourself and these two filthy urchins out of our sight. They offend us.' And, very rudely, he turned his back.

Tati had stopped being frightened. Anger was swelling up inside her like a bubble in a pan of boiling porridge. The bubble burst – and Tati shot forwards to confront the King.

'Call yourself a King?' she snapped. 'You're nothing but a rude, brainless bully. That's all you can do, is it? – smash things up, destroy things, kill trees! Snigger at people who need your help! You're pathetic! Well, let me tell you, Mr King – I don't like your sort either. You offend Us! Come on, Daio, it's time we went home.'

Angrily, she turned her own back on the flabbergasted courtiers and flounced away. There was a long moment of appalled silence. And then the King began to grow. He swelled and he swelled until he filled the entire sky, and as he grew he changed colour and shape until he was an immense storm-cloud, inky-black and threatening, with yellow agate eyes. His wrath gathered within him. And then the storm unleashed its fury on Tati and Daio and Cern.

Everywhere went black. The sunlight vanished. The green valley, the tents and the people seemed to disintegrate around them and fall away to a vast distance in a spinning, whirling void. The hurricane tore at them with giant hands and the thunder deafened them.

Cern grabbed both children and lifted them onto his shoulders.

'Hold tight!' he shouted above the clamour of the storm. He sprang into the air – and suddenly he wasn't in man-shape any more: he was a giant stag, galloping ahead of the gale.

125

126

The storm screeched its fury all round them as they fled. Bolts of lightning streaked past, singeing the stag's rough coat. Thunderclaps were so loud and so close they seemed to be exploding inside their heads. The hurricane tossed them this way and that until none of them could tell for certain which way was up ... Tati and Daio shut their eyes in terror and clutched the stag's mane for dear life. Cern galloped on.

Slowly, Cern drew ahead of the storm. The noise grew fainter, the wind died away and at last their headlong flight steadied to a canter. Tati and Daio opened their eyes.

Below them, under the peaceful stars, lay their own valley, with the lights of the town a yellow blur in the distance and the hills rising like black velvet out of the smudged tangles of the trees. They were home.

'What'll happen when he gets here?' Tati asked fearfully.

'He won't,' Cern told her reassuringly. 'His rages are terrible while they last, but he soon forgets what caused them.'

The great stag circled over Nant-y-Ceirw, and then came gently to earth in the one patch of darkness amongst all the brightly-lit streets. They were in the playground of the primary school. Cern threw back his massive, antlered head and bayed with the sound of trumpets. Every door in the school swung open.

'Now!' said Cern – and the bwganod scrambled off his back. They flew to the Nature Room. The lid of the cake tin was lying on the floor, and Bwganbabi, cross and red-faced from crying, was just starting to crawl out of his prison. Tati and Daio picked him up and hugged him, and he tangled his fingers painfully in their hair and scolded them loudly in baby-talk. He was very wet.

'Smelly, too,' said Daio, wrinkling his nose.

'At least he's in one piece,' said Tati thankfully.

127

They carried him outside in triumph to where the great
stag waited, pawing the ground and snorting.

It was a short flight this time. In less than a minute they
were circling the wood and coming in to land in the glade
where the Bwganhouse grew.

When it saw them, the Bwganhouse shuddered all over
with joy. The door burst open and a whole crowd of people
erupted into the glade: Mami and Dadi, Naino and Taid
and Dewin and Seamus, all talking at the tops of their
voices and jostling each other in their eagerness to welcome
the children home.

'My baby!' said Mami – and rushed to take Bwganbabi
from Daio's arms. 'Oh, Tati! Oh, Daio!' – and suddenly they
were all three being hugged and kissed and cried over.

The stag shimmered and became Cern the man, towering over the bwganod like a great oak tree burnished with red gold.

And when the grown-ups saw who it was that had brought the children home, there was a sudden, awed silence in the glade. For once, even Seamus had nothing to say. Everybody's jaw dropped, and then everybody (even Bwgantaid) bowed very low.

Dadi floated forwards. 'My Lord Cern,' he said, sounding utterly thunderstruck, 'was it you who rescued the children?'

Cern smiled down at Tati and Daio, and rested one hand lightly on each curly head.

'Only at the end,' he said. 'You've got a pair of brave youngsters here. Don't scold them, I beg of you. They've won through perils that have made warriors' hearts faint with fear. But they're safe now, and that's all that matters.'

'Well, now, didn't I tell yez all they'd be fine?' said Seamus.

Mami made a deep, graceful curtsey and took charge. 'Come inside, my Lord. We're not very grand, as you well know, but I'm sure you must be weary after your flight.'

Cern smiled. 'A cup of your cowslip wine would be very pleasant,' he admitted. 'And yes, I am a bit tired. It's hard work, flying ahead of the King of the West.'

They all filed inside the Bwganhouse again, Mami leading the way with Cern and the rest following. The Bwganhouse made itself into a palace for Cern, and the magic stones shone so brightly that the whole house seemed to be full of sunlight. Tati and Daio went in last of all, with Bwgantaid.

'Who *is* he?' Daio hissed in Bwgantaid's ear. 'How come you all bow to him like that? And how do you know him so well?'

'Don't you *know*?' Taid sounded quite shocked.

'No, why should we?' Tati said indignantly. 'We just met him, that's all. Nobody told us anything.'

'Well, you'd better mind your manners, then, hadn't you? That's Cernunnos, that is. Arglwydd y Goedwig – Lord of the Wood. All trees everywhere are in his care, and all bwganod. He's chief amongst the Great Ones, except for the winds, and the ocean.'

Their mouths dropped open. 'Blimey,' said Daio.

Inside the Bwganhouse Cern didn't behave in the least like the Lord of all the Trees. He sipped cowslip wine and laughed and chatted and thanked Naino for the cakes and fruit she brought him, just like a polite ordinary bwgan. Of course, the story of Tati and Daio's adventures had to be told right down to the last detail. Seamus, in particular, was horrified.

'Save us, ye might have been killed! I should have kept my big mouth shut, so I should!'

'But we did it, Seamus,' Tati told him. 'We weren't killed, and we got Bwganbabi back again, and that's why you helped us!'

'They did us proud, the pair of them,' said Dewin warmly. He didn't mind at all that his lovely circlet had been given to a Troll.

Dadi, however, was looking very serious. 'I don't want to spoil things – but you do realise, don't you, that this entire mess happened because of that human you've been visiting?'

Tati and Daio gasped. Gramps! In all the excitement, they'd completely forgotten about Gramps's magic show. Their hearts sank. Poor Gramps! He must have been waiting there in the hospital ward for ages. He'd be so disappointed. No good trying to sneak away now – not with Cern and everybody here.

They braced themselves for the inevitable telling-off. Judging from the look on Dadi's face, they'd be lucky if they got off with a bad scolding. And both Dadi and Mami were practically certain to insist that they promised never to visit humans again. So they'd never get the chance to explain to Gramps why they'd let him down so badly. He'd be hurt, and sad. It wasn't fair ...

'Don't you think you should have told us weeks ago?' Dadi said. 'Didn't you know you were breaking the Rules?'

There was nothing to be said. Tati and Daio just hung their heads.

Mami saw their faces, and laid a consoling hand on Dadi's arm. 'Don't be too hard on them, love. They're young, they're inquisitive – and the world's a very different place these days. When we were their age, there weren't any humans in this valley. Now they're everywhere, and you can't ignore them any more.'

Cern nodded his shaggy russet head. 'Humans,' he said thoughtfully, and sighed. 'Humans are a problem we haven't even begun to tackle yet. In the old days, humans got along with us and we got along with them, more or less. But recently, things have changed. They've forgotten us. They've forgotten that they're part of Earth, just like trees. They've become greedy and thoughtless, they burn and pollute and destroy. They've started to behave like spoilt children who smash up the presents their mother gives them, and bully her, and kick and hurt her. Perhaps the time has come for us to teach them once again how to love and care for their mother the Earth, just as we do.'

Everybody was quiet for a while after that.

Tati said timidly, 'So ... can we go and see Gramps after all, and explain?'

Dadi glanced at Cern, who nodded encouragingly.

'I suppose so,' said Dadi. 'A promise is a promise, after all.'

'We can't give a magic show, though, can we?' Daio said forlornly. 'We gave everything away, except for Dewin's butterflies.'

Cern's eyes were glinting with very bwgan-like mischief. 'Oh, I wouldn't be too sure about that, if I were you.'

'What d'you mean?' Tati demanded.

Cern's smile broadened. 'Why don't we *all* go?' he suggested.

15

An Amazing Party

Gramps was sitting up in bed when Tati and Daio arrived in the hospital ward. He was looking more than usually grumpy.

'Bout time, too,' he grumbled. 'Forgot all about it, did you?'

'No!' said Tati fiercely. 'We just got held up, that's all.'

Everybody else in the ward was lying down, half-asleep. The lights were turned down low. At the far end of the room a brighter light shone through a small square window. A nurse was sitting on the other side of the window, writing in a book and glancing up every now and again to check on the patients.

'Where's this entertainment, then?' said Gramps.

Right on cue, Cern and Mamibwgan and Dadibwgan and Bwganbabi, and Naino and Taid and Dewin and Seamus all appeared in the ward together. Cern lifted his hand – and the magic began.

The wall between the old men's ward and the old ladies' ward shimmered and vanished. The overhead lights came on, and turned golden and dappled like sunlight shining through young leaves in spring. The flowers in the vases started growing very fast, and sprouted long tendrils which climbed the walls and over the ceiling until the whole room was a mass of blossom. All the old ladies and all the old men suddenly sat up and sprang out of bed and began to put on their dressing-gowns. Their cheeks were pink and their eyes sparkled.

The nurse in her little room kept on writing in her book, and didn't seem to have noticed a thing.

Then Cern produced a fiddle out of nowhere, and he and Seamus began to play: happy, jiggy music which made you want to dance. Chattering like starlings, the old ladies and the old men pushed the beds back against the walls to make a big space in the middle – and the next moment, everybody was dancing. The old people skipped and hopped and whirled each other round and did fancy steps as though they were sixteen again, instead of nearly ninety. The old ladies capered like fauns, and the old men clapped the beat.

Tati and Daio stared, goggle-eyed.

'Fancy them being able to jump about like that!' Daio said, awed. 'Even Gramps – look! And he hasn't coughed once!'

'It's Cern,' Tati said. 'He's made them all young again.'

Then Dewin appeared, laughing, and grabbed Tati's hand to whirl her away into the dance, while Naino did the same with Daio.

Between the dances food and drink appeared on the tables, and there were other entertainments. Cern played his fiddle and Mami sang a song, and everybody clapped like mad. They could all see the bwganod and their friends, and none of the humans seemed to think it was at all peculiar. Then Dewin got up and did some marvellous conjuring tricks with his butterflies, and everyone oohed and aahed and clapped all over again. Three old ladies and three old men did a clog dance with the whole room cheering them on. One old man recited 'Albert and the Lion' in a funny accent and made them all laugh. Then Seamus got up and sang a very funny song about an old lady who wrote a letter and addressed it to 'My Son In Amerikay'.

Perhaps the best moment of all was when one of the oldest people present sang an ancient Welsh love-song in a sweet tenor voice and the whole audience joined in, very softly and reverently, in four-part harmony.

In between the dancing and the entertainments everybody got together in little groups to laugh and talk. Gramps and Bwgantaid found a corner to themselves and were deep in conversation for most of the evening. Gramps was actually beaming. Everybody made a fuss of Tati and Daio, and Bwganbabi got handed round from one old lady to another to be cuddled and petted.

'Where's Naino?' Tati asked Daio as they handed round refreshments (a job they always seemed to get landed with whenever there was a party).

Daio didn't know. They looked round, puzzled. Then Daio pointed. 'Isn't that her over there?'

Naino and four other (human) old ladies were sitting in a huddle at one end of the room. Whatever they were talking about, it was obviously very funny, because shrieks of uproarious laughter kept coming from that direction. Every time the laughter died down one or other of the old ladies would lean forward and begin talking, and four heads would bend closer to listen – and you could tell from the expressions on their faces that what she was saying was extremely funny and probably rather naughty. Then all five heads would lift up at the same moment in another peal of loud, cackling laughter until they were all rocking to and fro with mirth and holding their tummies and wiping their eyes. Then another old lady would lean forward and start talking, and the whole sequence would start all over again.

Seething with curiosity, Tati and Daio began to drift towards the group.

136

'Oh, no you don't.' Dadi and Mami planted themselves very firmly in their way. Dadi was grinning, and managing to look a bit shocked at the same time.

'Why, what are they *talking* about?'

'They're swopping recipes for nettle beer,' Mami said primly – though she, too, was laughing and looking rather pink.

Tati and Daio were baffled. 'What's so funny about nettle beer?'

They'd tasted some of Naino's famous nettle beer once, by accident, and they hadn't liked it at all. Afterwards, it had made them feel most peculiar.

'It's not the nettle beer so much,' Mami said carefully, 'it's what tended to happen to the people who drank it.'

'Oh,' said Tati.

There was another burst of raucous laughter from the end of the room.

'They're a bunch of wicked old ladies,' Dadi said. 'And your Naino's the worst of the lot.'

Just then Cern and Seamus struck up another tune, and the dancing started once more.

It was a wonderful party, and it went on for most of the night. The nurse sat peacefully in her little office and saw and heard nothing at all. No one else in that huge hospital had the faintest idea of what was happening in the old people's wards.

Right at the end Mami and Dadi danced the last waltz together, all by themselves in the middle of the floor. When the music stopped they turned and bowed, and everybody cheered and clapped.

They all hurried to push the beds back to their proper places. The flowers shrank to their normal size. The bright sunlight faded and the dim bluish night-lights came on instead, making the whole room look dingy and shabby.

The wall reappeared between the two wards. Wearily now, but very happily, the old people got back into their beds.

Tati and Daio went to say good night to Gramps.

'Good party?' said Daio.

'Oh, aye,' Gramps said sleepily. 'Champion. Champion.' And he smiled warmly at them both.

When Cern and Dewin and Seamus and the bwganod left the hospital, the humans were all asleep, and smiling.

'Wonder if they'll remember?' Tati murmured.

'Some of them will,' said Cern. 'Some won't, of course, or they'll think it was a dream. But they'll all be happier and livelier, after tonight.'

Mostyn Close was dark under the stars and utterly silent. In the two houses halfway along the close David and Eleri were sound asleep. They'd managed to get home safely and sneak back indoors before any of the grown-ups had realised they'd been out. Then they'd hung around, waiting anxiously for some message from the bwganod.

At bedtime, they'd both tried their hardest to stay awake, just in case there was news of Bwganbabi. But nothing had happened, and in the end their eyes had simply refused to stay open any longer.

Suddenly, and at exactly the same moment, they both woke up.

There was a light outside their windows – a pale, moving, shimmering sort of light which wasn't street lamps or moonlight or a car turning round ... Somehow they both felt compelled to get out of bed. They each padded to the window and looked out. And there they saw an astonishing sight.

A gigantic stag was hovering in the air alongside their windows. On its back sat a leprechaun and a dwarf. All around it floated bwganod, gleaming with pale rainbow colours in the starlight, their long hair streaming behind them as they flew.

Trembling with excitement, David and Eleri opened their windows wide and leaned out. All the bwganod were smiling and waving.

'We made it!' Tati called. 'Bwganbabi's safe!' – and there he was, being held up proudly in the arms of a beautiful bwgan-lady.

'See you around, okay?' said Daio.

The giant stag surged forwards and galloped away through the air. At the end of the Close it leapt above the rooftops and was gone, leaving a trail of silver in the sky.

The sequel to *Who's Afraid of the Bwgan-Wood?*:

The Scary Monster Clean-Up Gang

by Anne Lewis

More Bwgan adventures for children from 7 to 11 years old

*Strange and scary things can sometimes happen to people
who wander through the Old Ironworks, especially at dusk
or in the dark. Because if humans are stupid enough to
build roads and towns and factories and big new estates
right next to where the Ancient Ones live – the least
you can expect is a bit of mischief now and again.
And sooner or later, there's bound to be trouble . . .*

The sly old swamp-witch, Gwrach y Rhibyn, meddles
with a powerful new spell, which she hopes will make
her Queen of the Wood. But the spell goes horribly
wrong. The whole town of Nant-y-Ceirw is trapped in
the thrall of the hideous Shadow of Don't Care and
the Bwganod of the Wood are in terrible danger.

It's up to their human friends – Gramps and David
and Eleri and Eleri's Nan – to rescue them.
Somehow they must defeat the Shadow.

But how can you fight magic?

ISBN 1 870 206 371   £3.95

Also in the award-winning *Bwgan-Wood* series:

The Dragonchild

by Anne Lewis

Something is wrong with the magic.
Someone is feeding on it.

A dragon egg was stolen by elves and lost in
Nant-y-Ceirw 500 years before. Now it's hatching, in a
world where it doesn't belong. The town and the wood
will be destroyed, and the dragon itself will die, unless
David, Eleri, Brynmor, Tati and Daio, can save them.

But Time and humans mean nothing to elves.
They'll do anything to cover up the theft.
The bwganod and the children are up against cleverer,
more powerful enemies than any they've faced before.
Their whole world is at stake.

All they have is their own courage
– and a Moon-horse.

ISBN 1 870206 55 X   £3.95

ABOUT HONNO

Honno Welsh Women's Press was set up in 1986 by a group of women who felt strongly that women in Wales needed wider opportunities to see their writing in print and to become involved in the publishing process. Our aim is to publish books by, and for, women of Wales, and our brief encompasses fiction, poetry, children's books, autobiographical writing and reprints of classic titles in English and Welsh.

Honno is registered as a community co-operative and so far we have raised capital by selling shares at £5 a time to over 350 interested women all over the world. Any profit we make goes towards the cost of future publications. We hope that many more women will be able to help us in this way. Shareholders' liability is limited to the amount invested, and each shareholder, regardless of the number of shares held, will have her say in the company and a vote at the AGM. To buy shares, to buy books directly, to be added to our database of authors or to receive further information about forthcoming publications, please write to Honno:

'Ailsa Craig',
Heol y Cawl,
Dinas Powys,
Bro Morgannwg
CF64 4AH.